The Fury of Zococa

Roy Patterson

A Black Horse Western

ROBERT HALE

ISBN 978-0-7198-2064-9

The Crowood Press
The Stable Block
Crowood Lane
Ramsbury
Marlborough
Wiltshire SN8 2HR

www.crowood.com

Robert Hale is an imprint
of The Crowood Press

Typeset by
Derek Doyle & Associates, Shaw Heath
Printed and bound in Great Britain by
CPI Group (UK) Ltd, Croydon, CR0 4YY

PROLOGUE

Luis Santiago Rodrigo Vallencio was a flamboyant character who had relished becoming an outlaw and had worked very hard at achieving his ambition. Yet few knew that was his real name as everyone knew him as Zococa, the one who favoured his left side. A hundred crimes had been attributed to the left-handed bandit over the years, even though he had not committed any of them.

Zococa relished being famous and also enjoyed the excitement of outwitting the law on both sides of the border despite knowing the cost of failing was his life. He had been branded the most ruthless of all his chosen breed and rode with a hefty price upon his head.

Yet none of this mattered to the handsome bandit as he led his mute companion, the enormous

Apache Tahoka, into the depths of a remote canyon with towering sand coloured walls.

The Indian pulled back on his reins and raised his massive right hand and then pointed at the ground. Zococa eased his pinto stallion to the side of Tahoka and stared at the smooth sand. He glanced at the trouble warrior.

'What do you see, my little one?' he asked as the powerful black and white stallion pulled at his reins. 'I see nothing but white sand, *amigo*.'

Tahoka turned his cruelly maimed face and looked at his friend. He spoke swiftly with his fingers and hands and then dismounted and knelt.

Zococa looped his leg over the black mane of his elegant horse and slid to the ground. He held his beaded reins firmly and moved to the side of the concerned Apache.

'You are worrying me, little one,' Zococa admitted as he knelt beside his gigantic pal. 'There is nothing here but sand. What do you see?'

Tahoka placed the palms of both hands on the hot sand and then lowered his ear on to the white crystals. For a moment he remained perfectly still and then rose up on to his knees. Even a face covered in vicious scars could not conceal the look of concern from his comrade.

Zococa watched his friend for a few moments

and then spoke out again. 'What is it, Tahoka? What has my *amigo* noticed?'

Tahoka jumped back to his feet and stared along the sun-baked canyon like an eagle seeking its prey. He shook his mane of long black hair and then grabbed his saddle horn and threw his large body up on to the back of his mount. As he gathered up his reins he looked down at the famed bandit and gestured with his hands.

Zococa read the silent words and frowned.

'Are you sure, my little one?' he asked as he quickly mounted the pinto. 'There is trouble ahead? What kind of trouble?'

The Apache warrior spoke again with his hands.

Zococa raised his eyebrows in surprise. 'You say that you hear the cries of those who are injured?'

Tahoka nodded and pointed at the shimmering heat haze ahead of them. Then he told his watchful partner that there was a ferocious fight being waged somewhere down the long winding canyon.

Zococa gripped his reins and rose in his stirrups. He gritted his teeth and looked at his faithful friend.

'Come, my little one,' he said firmly. 'We must ride fast to help those who are under attack.'

Both horsemen urged their mounts into full flight. Within a mere few beats of their hearts, the two riders were at full gallop. The sound of their horses' hoofs echoed all around them as they whipped the tails of their mounts and thundered along the high banked canyon.

Then as both riders were racing between the towering canyon walls, they began to hear the sound of gunfire growing louder with every stride of their mounts. Zococa glanced across at his grim-faced friend and nodded. He did not understand how Tahoka could do what he did but the Apache warrior had never been proven wrong.

It was as though the giant Indian was able to sense trouble even when it was not evident to anyone else. The pair of horsemen guided their mounts between giant boulders and deeper into the sickening haze.

Then suddenly both riders heard the unmistakable sound of rifle fire. This time it was different though. This time the bullet was aimed at them.

Zococa was first to react as a white hot taper carved a way through the haze and ricocheted off the canyon wall. The bandit urgently dragged back on his reins and stopped the pinto stallion as the Apache slowed his mount beside him.

A second shot came through the molten air. This time it was closer. Far too close. The stallion shuddered beneath Zococa and then reared up as though defiantly fighting their unseen attacker.

Tahoka swung his mount around and stared at the bandit as Zococa fought valiantly to control the stallion. Then another ear-splitting rifle shot rang out from somewhere along the canyon.

This time the bullet seemed to find its target.

There was a sickening sound as the bandit flew backwards from his rearing mount. Zococa spun like a top and crashed into the dusty ground beside the mute Apache's horse.

Tahoka gave out a silent cry as he stared down at his motionless partner. Feverishly, Tahoka pulled his rifle from its scabbard, cranked its mechanism and fired off into the swirling heat haze.

ONE

The Apache had nearly exhausted his ammunition as he sat astride the high-shouldered horse when he noticed his dazed friend suddenly throw himself over onto his knees. The irate Indian dropped from the back of his mount and leaned down to help the young Mexican. His large hand gripped Zococa under the armpit and helped the stunned bandit to his feet.

'What happened, my little rhinoceros?' Zococa coughed as he patted his aching chest in search of the bullet he knew had knocked him off his ornate saddle.

Tahoka used his enormous body to shield the bandit from further injury. With the Winchester in his firm grip, he glanced back over his shoulder as Zococa kept looking for the blood which he felt sure should be pumping from his body.

There was no blood.

The shots ceased as quickly as they had started. Suddenly the canyon fell silent and the massive warrior finally turned to face his pal. The Apache was as confused as the bandit as he gazed at him.

Zococa then found a bullet hole in the black jacket. He pushed his finger through the hole and then looked blankly at the Apache. The famed bandit pulled the jacket away from his shirt and ran the palm of his hand across the cotton. Although the shirt was unmarked, Zococa winced. His fingers swiftly unbuttoned the shirt and stared at his bruised chest.

'I was right,' Zococa said. 'I was shot.'

Tahoka quickly talked with his hands in search of an explanation. There seemed to be no possible way that a bullet could hit anyone in the chest but only leave a bruise.

Zococa pushed his sombrero off his head and allowed it to rest upon his back. His eyes stared at the sand and then he noticed the sun glinting off something at his feet. He leaned over and scooped up the buckled lump of lead. He showed it to Tahoka.

'Look, *amigo*.' Zococa grinned. 'The bullet just bounced off my chest. I am tougher than I thought.'

Tahoka gave a snort and then pulled his partner's jacket away from his lean form and then slid out the thick silver cigar case from the inside pocket and rammed it under Zococa's nose.

Zococa raised his eyebrows and took the case from the Apache and looked at its dented lid. A rifle bullet had hit the silver case and bounced off. Although not powerful enough to pass through the solid silver case it still had enough force behind it to knock its target off the back of his rearing pinto stallion.

Zococa shrugged and tossed the bullet over his shoulder and returned the silver case to his jacket pocket.

'Is it not fortunate that I stole that cigar case, my little one?' he asked before walking to where his faithful mount was waiting. He grabbed the saddle horn and stepped into his stirrup. Zococa mounted the muscular animal in one well-rehearsed action and then moved to the side of the awaiting Apache brave.

Zococa looked up to the top of the jagged canyon walls which loomed above them to both sides. The shots had come from up there, Zococa thought to himself. Yet whoever had done the shooting in a vain bid to stop them advancing further along the canyon, was now gone.

The Apache slid his rifle back into its leather scabbard and grabbed the mane of his mount.

Tahoka swung up on to his horse and gathered his reins in his powerful hands. He pointed ahead of them and reminded Zococa of the cries which he could still detect. He frantically spoke to the Mexican with his agile hands.

'You are right, my brave one,' Zococa agreed as he nodded to the warrior. 'There is someone in big trouble and we have to help them.'

Both riders lashed their long leathers across the backs of their mounts and jolted the powerful horses into action once again. Defying the unknown dangers which had almost claimed one of their lives, they raced through the heat haze at thunderous pace.

They were both determined that nothing could stop them this time. Not even the devilish rifle bullets of their unseen enemy would slow their progress.

TWO

The shimmering heat haze parted like the biblical Red Sea as Zococa and Tahoka drew closer to the end of the high walled canyon. Both horsemen could see a twisting trail which led from the very floor of the canyon up to the very top of the canyon's high walls. Zococa noticed that a cloud of dust still hung over the rough ground all the way up the steep incline.

'The gunman must have ridden up there from here, Tahoka,' he announced as he steadied his pinto. 'That is where he shot at us from.'

The Apache nodded in agreement as they pressed on. For a few endless moments the riders searched the surrounding rocks for the sniper who had slowed their progress. Yet the mysterious

14

gunman had gone.

The two sturdy horses had only just travelled a couple of hundred yards when something caught their masters' attention just beyond a group of massive boulders that littered the area.

The Apache pointed ahead at the remains of a covered wagon which lay amid blood-stained sand. Its team of horses had broken free of their restraints and were long gone and its wheels hung from broken axles. Tahoka drew his long leathers to his muscular chest and stopped his lathered-up horse. The alert brave stared at the wagon and listened intently.

Zococa walked his horse toward the pitiful sight which faced him. The blood which was baking beneath the unyielding sun was spread out from the shattered driver's box. It sparkled in the overhead sun. Zococa glanced around the scene of destruction as his fertile imagination pieced together what had happened here. To the famed bandit it was clear that someone had bushwhacked the wagon, causing its stricken driver to lose control. The wagon had collided with the boulders and then come to a rest where it now festered.

Only as his horse paused and snorted did the Mexican throw his right leg over the animal's black mane and slide to the ground.

Zococa was as silent as his companion as he walked toward the stationary wreckage. Every one of his honed senses was alert as he studied the broken wooden vehicle before him. Its canvas covering and metal hoops were strewn across the ground and spread out in every direction.

The bandit headed toward the blood for that was where he knew he would find the victim of this outrage. Zococa carefully stepped between the scarlet gore toward the front of the prairie schooner.

The battle which his companion had heard a few moments earlier was etched into the otherwise pristine sand. The front of the wagon was filled with bullet holes. Blood had spewed out in all directions from the overturned body of the wagon as evidence of what still lay undetected beneath the crippled canvas, which flapped in the blinding sunlight.

Zococa glanced up at Tahoka who had dismounted.

The large Apache walked like a panther around the broken vehicle until he was at the side of the bandit. He placed a hand on Zococa's shoulder, pointed at the canvas and then moved toward it.

16

The famed bandit followed on his friend's heels. As both men reached the shattered wooden side of the wagon they heard the groaning come from beneath the loose fabric.

'Someone is still alive, Tahoka,' Zococa said as he knelt down and started to drag the wagon's covering away from the middle of the busted body of the vehicle. 'Quickly, we must find whoever it is that is making so much noise.'

Both men worked feverishly and dragged the large expanse of canvas away from what was concealed beneath its grey bulk. The Apache and the bandit frantically toiled until the blood covered face of a badly injured man suddenly met their eyes.

'Thank the Lord,' the injured man groaned feebly.

'Do not move, *señor*,' Zococa urged as he studied the badly injured man.

The bandit reasoned that the injured man was somewhere in his thirties. It was obvious that the crash had broken many of his bones. Yet it was the two bullets which were causing the blood to pump from his broken body. It was clear to Zococa by the placement of the bullet holes that he had been the bushwhacker's target.

'I drove the wagon around the corner and then

all hell broke out,' the man mumbled. 'I lost the leathers and the next thing I recall is crashing.'

Zococa carefully placed an arm around the broken man and attempted to calm him down.

'Do not fret yourself, *amigo*,' Zococa said as he cradled the badly injured man in his arms, as the knowing eyes of Tahoka studied the injuries more carefully.

Tahoka looked straight into the face of his companion. It was clear to the bandit what his silent friend was conveying in his own unique way. The Apache was telling Zococa that the injuries were beyond their limited knowledge of medicine. There was nothing they could do apart from wait for death to claim him.

Zococa nodded his silent agreement as the large Apache moved away from them to continue his search of the destruction.

'M-my daughter,' the man gasped as his fingers clawed at Zococa's jacket. 'Find my little daughter.'

The bandit and the Apache brave looked at one another in stunned horror. Zococa then pressed his face close to the ear of the injured man he cradled.

'Your daughter?' he repeated quietly. 'Where is your daughter, *amigo*? Give us your address and Tahoka and I shall go to her.'

The pained expression looked into Zococa's troubled face as his fingers gripped the Mexican more firmly.

'You don't understand,' he croaked in urgency. 'Little Mary is here somewhere. We were going to town. I was going to buy her a doll for her birthday.'

Zococa looked at Tahoka and indicated for the warrior to search in earnest. The Apache nodded and carefully stepped over the running board and continued his search amid the debris.

'Do not worry, my friend,' the handsome Mexican urged as he wiped blood from the face of the stricken man. 'We will find your little Mary.'

Every word he spoke was matched with his eyes following the lumbering Tahoka as he continued to carefully make his way through the wreckage in search for the daughter of the injured man. As his large fingers peeled shattered lumber aside the mute warrior suddenly stopped.

He looked over his broad shoulder back at the Mexican. His expression was grim.

Zococa looked back at the man in his arms. He was dying and they both knew it. The bandit could not understand why anyone would choose to attack a covered wagon when there were plenty of more valuable targets to unleash their bullets at.

19

'Who shot you, *amigo*?'

The man was fighting a losing battle with death as he focused on the elegant bandit.

'Joe Barnaby of Diablo has bin trying to buy my small holding for months.' He gasped before continuing. 'But me and little Mary buried her mother there after the fever claimed her. I couldn't sell up. It would break Mary's heart.'

Zococa focused on the man. 'This Joe Barnaby bushwhacked you, *amigo*? Is that it?'

Somehow the man shook his head. 'No, not Barnaby. He's rich but he's also a coward. He must have hired someone to do his killing for him.'

'Are you sure of this?' Zococa asked as he watched the Apache bend down and scoop the tiny form of the man's daughter up in his mighty arms. 'Are you sure that this Barnaby paid someone to kill you?'

'As sure as I can be, friend.' A trickle of blood ran from the corner of his mouth. 'I recognized the varmint who opened up on us. He's a paid killer. His name's Holt Danvers. He rides a grey and hires his guns out to whoever got his price.'

Zococa ran his hand over the brow of the stricken man.

'There is no worse animal than a hired gun,

señor.' He sighed as he watched Tahoka carefully climb out of the belly of the wagon with the young girl in his massive arms. He was about to speak again when he noticed that the man's head was slumped into his chest. Delicately Zococa touched the neck of the man but he could not detect a pulse.

He gently eased the lifeless body down on to the sand and then rose to his full height and crossed to where Tahoka stood like a giant statue with the small girl in his arms.

The bandit stared at the youngster and then looked into the hooded eyes of the Apache.

'Is little Mary with the angels, Tahoka?' he reluctantly asked the warrior.

To his surprise Tahoka shook his head. Zococa brushed her dark brown hair off her bloodied face and then touched her neck. His fingertips detected a faint pulse. He patted the shoulder of his friend and nodded firmly.

'I shall get the horses, *amigo*,' he enthused. 'There is a mission five miles from here. We shall take Mary there and let the brothers tend her.'

As the large Apache watched his partner leading their mounts toward him he felt the tiny girl move in his arms. The bandit swiftly mounted and then held his arms out to Tahoka. He carefully cradled the girl in his arms as Tahoka threw himself on to the back of his own mount.

The bandit poked his moccasins into his stirrups and pointed at the hoof tracks which led up to the very top of the canyon walls. The Apache knew that the perpetrator of this horrific slaughter was probably less than a mile away from them and wanted to give chase. He frantically gestured with his hands but Zococa had more important things on his mind as he held the fragile child in his arms. The bandit shook his head.

'Come, little elephant. We have to get Mary to where she can be helped.' Zococa gently turned his pinto and started the stallion in the direction where he knew he would find the remote mission. 'After we deliver our precious cargo we have to head to a place called Diablo. There we will find the man who did this and also the hombre who paid him.'

The brutalized face of Tahoka knew that the bandit was right. The injured young girl was barely clinging to life. He nodded and turned his mount and then trailed his companion out into the whispering heat haze toward the mission of San Gabriel.

The mute warrior was willing to wait until they had fulfilled the first part of their endeavour. But once Mary was delivered into the caring hands of the monks, Tahoka vowed to administer his own brand of vengeance.

THREE

Holt Danvers had not wasted one second of the time it had taken him to reach the vast open desert since he had fulfilled his agreement with Joe Barnaby and ambushed Frank Carver in the desolate canyon. Danvers was a prized asset to his cowardly paymasters who either held grudges or simply allowed their greed to overrule any morals they might once have held.

The brutal hired gun showed his grey no mercy as he continued to drive his razor sharp spurs into its flanks and drive the powerful mount on to his next unsuspecting victim.

Few men had ever had a chance against the brilliant gun skills that Danvers possessed. Those who tried to bring the weight of the law down upon him fared no better than his chosen prey. They

24

died with lethal accuracy. There was only one thing which the deadly gunman was an expert at and that was destroying anyone or anything that stood before him.

The horse beneath his expensive saddle stopped as its reins were dragged back. A cloud of dust rose from its hoofs as the powerful grey came to an abrupt halt.

As the dust cleared, Danvers stared through it and the shimmering heat haze to the town that stood upon the distant horizon. The bright rays of the blistering sun danced across the array of structures. It was like looking at a diamond necklace.

A twisted grin etched his heartless face as he held his long leathers in his gloved hands and balanced in his stirrups.

'Silver Creek.' Danvers hissed the town's name like a rattler warning the unwary of an impending strike. He slowly lowered himself back down upon the saddle and placed a long black cigar between his lips. 'Once I'm through there I'll have earned myself a pretty bonus.'

His left hand pulled a match from his vest pocket and scratched it across the horn of his saddle. He sucked in the strong smoke and then blew the match out before tossing it aside.

Danvers had long felt that he was indestructible

but in truth he seldom played fairly with those he had been paid to kill. When the hired gunman unleashed his brutal weaponry upon his unsuspecting victims it was usually by bushwhacking or any other devious device that came to hand. His putrid mind thought about the next kill he had to execute before he could head back to the lawless Diablo. The horse beneath him was snorting as he inhaled more and more smoke. Then he looked back over his wide shoulder at the golden coloured rocks still bathed in the merciless sun. He wondered who it had been that he had been forced to waste bullets upon.

'Who were them two *hombres* that were riding down the canyon?' Danvers asked himself as he recalled the sight of the Mexican bandit and his faithful companion as they rode down the canyon in a vain attempt to help Frank Carver. His grin widened as he thought about the sight of the Mexican horseman being knocked from his saddle by his deadly accurate rifle bullet.

'At least I killed one of them bastards. He sure learned the hard way that it don't pay to poke your nose into business that don't concern you.'

With the cigar gripped between his teeth, he looped his leg over his saddle-bags and dropped to the ground. Still chuckling, Danvers then reached up and pulled his canteen free. He dropped his hat onto the sand and then unscrewed the stopper of the canteen. He filled the bowl of his hat with the liquid and then replaced its stopper.

His narrowed eyes remained glued on the small settlement perched on the shimmering horizon. He knew it would take him at least an hour to ride to Silver Creek and do what had to be done.

Danvers tightened the stopper and then hung the canteen's leather straps over the saddle horn. He sucked more smoke into his lungs.

'At this rate I should get back to Diablo long before sundown,' he told himself as he checked his cinch strap. 'I'll have me plenty of time to bed a couple of whores before midnight as long as the next critter on my list dies easy and don't put up a fight.'

Danvers reached down into his trail coat pocket and pulled a small black covered book from its depths. He slid a small pencil from its spine and licked its tip as he located the page with names upon it. The book was filled with his previous victims and the price he had demanded to execute them.

He scratched the name of Frank Carver out and then smiled to himself at the other name just below it.

'One down and one to go,' he muttered before returning the pencil to the book's spine and then dropping it back into the coat pocket. 'It sure is profitable in these parts.'

The grey finished its meagre ration of water and raised its head. Danvers plucked his Stetson off the sand and beat the damp hat against his leg before returning it to his head.

The hired gunman checked his arsenal of weapons and then placed the palm of his hand upon the saddle horn. He poked a boot toe into a stirrup, hoisted his long lean frame up and swung his leg over the wide saddle. No sooner had his right boot entered the stirrup than he spurred the tired horse.

The grey bolted into action as it vainly tried to outrun the spurs which had already stained its flesh with blood. As the horse gathered pace, the ruthless killer thought about the next name in his book. Danvers had no idea who Charlie Higgins was but it did not matter to him. He had a name, a place where he would find the owner of that name and that was all that ever mattered to him.

Danvers knew that he had to kill whoever belonged to the name in his book. Then he would get paid a bonus. There was nothing personal. It was simply business.

Brutal business but business.

The horse cut through the stale desert air as its master continued to thrust his spurs into its flanks. He thought about the name he had scrawled in the book and the hotel where he had been told he would find him.

He spat the remains of the cigar out and narrowed his eyes as they focused on the sun-baked settlement ahead of him. All he could think about was the kill.

For some heartless souls the taste of blood was more addictive than the most powerful of drugs. It was a taste which could never be satisfied, no matter how many times they feasted upon its gore. Danvers had made more money in the previous few years along the border than most men could earn in a dozen lifetimes, yet that was not what continued to drive him on.

It was the sickening pleasure of killing.

Danvers whipped the shoulders of the grey as it closed the distance between itself and the sun-bleached settlement. The high-shouldered horse obeyed its cruel master and thundered on toward its goal.

When Danvers had scratched out the name of Charlie Higgins in his book he would return to Diablo to the men who hired his lethal skills.

The sound of pounding hoofs filled the desert.

The grey mount defied its own exhaustion and galloped on toward Silver Creek as Danvers balanced in his stirrups like a charioteer of bygone times.

Death was coming to Silver Creek and it rode a grey.

FOUR

The old mission had stood in the desolate desert since the first Spanish missionaries had arrived in the arid terrain 200 years before. At that time there were no borders and only the various tribes of Indians to worry about. The mission had survived when so many others had failed. The monks had somehow tamed the sand and a plentiful supply of fresh spring water flourished where so many others had failed.

San Marie was a jewel in an otherwise ocean of sand.

Yet as time had passed the mission had become a place where only a few visited any more. Its once strong ties with the mother country had faded as the constantly altering politics had changed around San Marie.

For decades, only the nomadic Indians who had been converted to Christianity and wandering travellers visited the increasingly remote mission. In a hostile terrain, the sand-coloured structure never locked its gates or refused help to those who needed it.

The pair of horsemen truly needed the help of the brothers within San Marie as they steered their mounts toward the large mission. Zococa held the delicate young girl in his arms and allowed the massive Tahoka to guide them across the sun-baked sand toward the open gateway.

It was an oasis in an otherwise arid land.

San Marie gleamed in the blistering sun. Its bell-tower loomed above the rest of the mission like a beacon as the large Apache rode into the court-yard, leading the pinto stallion of his partner behind him.

No sooner had the horses come to a halt when monks emerged from various parts of the mission and went to the high-shouldered pinto stallion. It was as though they had known their help would be needed long before the arrival of the unusual pair of horsemen.

The monks carefully took the young female from the hands of the troubled bandit and rushed her into cool interior of the structure. Only then did Zococa relax briefly.

He dismounted and rubbed the grime from his face as Tahoka stepped down from his own horse and sat on the edge of the central fountain.

The Apache spoke with his large hands.

'*Sí, amigo*,' Zococa agreed as he walked to the sparkling water and scooped a handful to quench his thirst. 'The brothers will do everything they can. Mary could not be in better hands.'

Tahoka did not look convinced. He stared down at the sand and sighed heavily. It was not normal for the Apache to be so worried but the giant brave could not take his thoughts away from the tiny child.

Zococa placed a hand on the shoulder of the warrior.

'Do not worry, Tahoka,' he comforted. 'The brothers will do everything they can to bring the little one back to health. All we can do is have faith.'

Suddenly Tahoka rose up. His hands talked furiously.

Zococa nodded.

'I know, little one,' he agreed. 'The man that did this terrible thing will have to pay for his crimes.'

For the next few minutes the famed bandit explained what the child's dying father had told him. As the words sank into the mind of the Apache, the angrier Tahoka became. There were few things more dangerous than an angry Apache but a gigantic angry Apache was something even more daunting.

Zococa tried to calm his friend down but it seemed an impossible task. The warrior wanted vengeance for the little girl he had found inside the prairie schooner. It seemed that nothing else could satisfy his fevered rage.

Tahoka pleaded silently for them to head on out after the brutal bushwhacker but Zococa knew they had to let their horses rest. Both mounts needed water and food if they were to tackle the desert again.

'Listen to me, my little elephant,' Zococa said to the Apache. 'I agree with you but we must rest our horses before we can go anywhere. This desert will kill them before we can kill the black-hearted ambusher.'

Reluctantly Tahoka nodded.

The bandit patted his fuming cohort on the arm. 'We will go when the horses have rested, my little one. This I promise.'

Just as the words fell from Zococa's lips they both spotted the abbot walking out of the main building where Mary had been taken a few moments before.

Father Joseph looked ashen as he approached the two awaiting men beside the fountain. His face was etched with concern as he closed in on them.

'Is Mary still with us, Father?' Zococa asked the leader of the religious community fearfully. 'She has not died, has she?'

The abbot shook his head. 'She is fighting, my son. The brothers are doing everything they can.'

Zococa sighed heavily. 'I am most relieved, Father.'

The abbot stepped closer to the two men he had met several times. 'Tell me. Where did you find the child, Zococa?'

The bandit explained.

When the true horror had been conveyed the elderly monk shook his head in disbelief. His aged eyes looked at the pair of wanted men who stood before him. It was obvious to the abbot that neither Zococa nor Tahoka could simply forget this outrage.

'The Lord shall punish those responsible.' The abbot crossed himself and went to walk away.

'But the Lord is most busy, Father,' Zococa said as he rested his hands on his hips. 'I think Tahoka and I shall help Him.'

The old man knew it was pointless to argue with

the flamboyant bandit. Zococa was angry and even his smile could not conceal the truth from those who knew him.

'The brothers and I shall try and save the child, Zococa,' he said quietly. 'She is very badly hurt though. It is not looking too good but if she can survive the next twenty-four hours I believe she has a fighting chance.'

Tahoka gestured with his large hands.

'What did Tahoka say, Zococa?' Father Joseph asked.

'He said she is a fighter.' The bandit smiled.

'I pray that you are right, my son. I shall also pray that you will allow the Lord to deal with the person responsible.'

Zococa shrugged. 'But the Lord is needed here and will be kept very busy, Father. My little friend and I shall wait until our horses are rested and then we are headed to a devilish place where we will find the man who kills for money.'

'What is the name of this place, my son?'

'Diablo, Father,' Zococa answered. 'Diablo.'

'May the Lord go with you, my son.' The abbot lowered his head and continued walking back into the sand-coloured buildings. The Mexican turned and glanced at the massive Apache. Tahoka gave a grunt and spoke swiftly with his hands.

'*Sí*, my little elephant,' Zococa agreed. 'You are correct. There are many demons in the town called Diablo, but they are no match for us. They are not as angry as we are, *amigo*.'

The Apache warrior began unsaddling their mounts in preparation for the gruelling ride they would be forced to make when fed and rested. The Indian knew Zococa better than the young Mexican knew himself. Tahoka realized that he was chomping at the bit, just like he was, to find and punish the bushwhacker.

Zococa placed his ornate saddle on the edge of the fountain as the Apache poured a healthy ration of oats before both horses.

'When the horses have cooled down and the sun is a bit lower in the sky, we shall ride to Diablo,' Zococa said as he opened his buckled cigar case and extracted one. He placed it between his teeth and then ignited a match with his thumb nail.

Tahoka sat down beside the saddles and stared at the mission building. Just like his famous friend, he was concerned that even with the help of the Lord, the monks would be unable to help Mary.

He glanced at Zococa. His hooded eyes pleaded for reassurance but the bandit could not provide any.

Smoke filtered through Zococa's teeth as he

patted the muscular shoulder of his pal.

'Do not fret, little one,' he said. 'Whatever happens to the precious child, we will make sure that the stinking back-shooter never repeats his outrage.'

Tahoka nodded and stared at the sand between his feet. He had his own plans for Holt Danvers.

FIVE

The face of Holt Danvers was like the man himself. Scarred and twisted by his many encounters with those who had pitifully attempted to fight for their lives as they met their executioner. Even though the odds were stacked against them, and they had known that nothing could sway him from what he intended to do, most had vainly tried to fend off the coming of death.

Yet Danvers had shown them no mercy.

They had all been dispatched without a momentary thought for the right or wrong of their fate. Danvers had long ridden the borderland in search of his next pay day. He seldom had to travel far for his reputation had always ensured that whoever he hired out to, would be successful.

Ignoring the war that had raged between the

north and the south five years earlier, Danvers had become rich from his unequalled gun skills. Unlike the majority of his fellow men, he had never required any excuses to kill. All he required was the right price to be paid and then he would unleash his devilish gun fury.

Those who tried to stand in his way were cut down with equal distain. Nobody stopped Holt Danvers when he was committed to slaying his prey.

So it was as he rode toward Silver Creek as a dust storm swept across the region. The name of Charlie Higgins still waited to be erased from his book so that he could head back to the murky depths of Diablo. This time Danvers knew that he would be unable to ambush his victim. This time he would have to face the man he had been hired to kill.

Out from the swirling dust clouds, the deadly horseman suddenly appeared like the Grim Reaper seeking out his chosen target. The hundred or so townsfolk suddenly noticed the deathly rider as his grey mare walked into the heart of the remote community.

Covered in trail dust, Holt Danvers looked more like a phantom than the ruthless killer he actually was. Few had ever been able to work out where he

came from or where he went when he had com-
pleted his lethal handiwork. Even fewer remained
on the main street of Silver Creek as he steered his
grey toward the hotel where he had been informed
that the unsuspecting Higgins could be found.

Draped in a well-worn trail coat, his hunched
form gave no clue as to what his intentions were.
The horseman had never lived by the rules which
most men abided by and he intended dying the
same way.

He killed and then departed. There was never a
hint of guilt or worry that the law might catch up
with him one day. He did his work and then vanished.

Danvers dismounted outside the hotel and tied
his reins to the closest hitching pole. He raised his
head and stared from beneath his wide flat hat
brim at the people who scurried up and down the
street as was their daily ritual.

The tall figure pulled his gold watch from the
small pocket of his pants and then flicked its lid.
His cold eyes stared at the watch hands and then
he snapped the lid shut.

It was just still early enough for him to fulfil his
contract and return to Diablo. He tightened the
drawstring under his chin and then stepped up
onto the boardwalk. He reached down, turned the

brass door knob and entered the hotel.

The clerk looked up at the remarkable figure from behind his desk. His heart quickened as the dark soul closed the door against the flying sand and then turned.

Danvers's eyes burned across the lobby to the desk clerk and walked toward him. There was a calculated pace that the hired gunman always maintained. Danvers stopped and rested his hand upon the register as he quickly observed the interior of the hotel lobby.

The clerk slowly rose to his feet, lifted the pen from the blotter and dipped it into the ink well.

'Do you wanna register, mister? We got plenty of rooms.'

There was an ominous quiet in the dark figure as he loomed over the counter and stared into the face of the clerk. He pushed the brim of his hat up off his dust-caked features and narrowed his eyes on the man before him. Even before Danvers had opened his mouth it was as though he were daring the naïve hotel worker to try his luck.

'Nope.' Danvers shook his head slowly as his right hand pushed his trail coat over the grip of one of his holstered guns. 'I don't want a room.'

The desk clerk could not understand why anyone would enter the hotel if they did not require someplace to rest their bones. He studied the stranger and noted that Danvers was covered in at least fifty miles of trail grime. He leaned further forward.

'You don't wanna rent a room?' he asked. 'Then what do you want? We ain't got liquor or vittles. The only thing I have got is rooms.'

Danvers grabbed the face of the clerk and pressed his fingertips into its flesh.

'You got a varmint named Charlie Higgins staying here?' he rasped as if still chewing on the dust he had just ridden through. 'I'm told he's a short, fat fella. Is he staying here?'

The gunman released his grip. The clerk felt his jaw shaking as he stared into the unholy features that bore down upon him. He gave a frightened nod.

'He sure is,' the clerk answered.

Danvers looked angrily at the neatly dressed man across the desk from him. His fists clenched for a moment and he glanced up at the landing.

'Is he here now?' he growled.

A bead of sweat trailed down the face of the clerk as he nervously stood before the grim-faced man.

'Room twelve.' He gulped before asking, 'Is he a friend of yours?'

Again, Danvers shook his head. 'Is he in his room right now?' he said.

The clerk raised his eyebrows as he glanced at the staircase and then returned his attention to the gunman. He could not understand why this stranger was so interested in one of his guests.

'He sure is.' He nodded, pointing at the thread-bare carpet that barely covered the staircase steps. 'Higgins never rises until about three or four in the afternoon. He's a night owl. He likes to play poker until the roosters start belly-aching.'

Danvers held his hand out. 'Give me his room key.'

Without arguing, the clerk reached back and plucked a pass key off a hook and shakily handed it to the deadly killer before him.

Danvers's fingers curled around the key as he flicked the safety loop off his gun hammer and turned toward the stairs.

'I'm here to kill the bastard.'

'What?' the clerk croaked as the reality of the situation finally dawned on him.

'And if I was you I'd stay behind that desk until I'm finished,' Danvers said in a low whisper before glancing over his shoulder at the petrified man. 'Don't even think about running for the law.'

The clerk loosened his starched collar.

'I ain't the running kind, mister,' he said.

'Good,' Danvers snarled. 'Otherwise I'll have to kill you as well.'

The tall gunman started to make his way up to the second floor of the windswept hotel. The clerk watched in terror as he slowly sat back down upon his chair.

The sound of his spurs rang out like the tolling of bells as he slowly ascended to the landing, leaving a trail of dust in his wake. Room twelve was a mere ten strides from the top of the stairs. Danvers made short work of the distance and stopped. He pressed an ear against the door and could hear the sound of snoring.

Sleeping men were always easier to kill.

A cruel smile etched his face as he slid the key into the lock and carefully turned it. Danvers pushed the door inward and followed its progress into the room.

His spurs rang out as he strode to the end of the bed and stared at the fat man fighting with his dreams under the bedsheets.

Danvers drew his Peacemaker, cocked its hammer and then smashed its barrel across Higgins's leg. The startled figure awoke suddenly but before he could scream out in pain he felt the cold metal barrel pressed against his temple.

Higgins looked along the barrel and then focused on the scarred face of the deadly gunman.

'Who are you?' he asked.

The hired killer continued to stare down upon the half-naked man looking up at him.

'Is your name Higgins?' Danvers rasped. 'Charlie Higgins?'

There was no call for a reply. The expression on the rotund face betrayed Higgins. His eyes darted to the chair where his clothes were strewn over his gunbelt.

'My name's not Higgins,' the fat man protested weakly.

Danvers smiled.

For a brief moment Charlie Higgins actually thought that the professional killer believed him. He gave a pathetic grin and then Danvers squeezed the trigger of his gun. The room rocked to the deafening crescendo. Blood splattered across the bed and up the wall.

Gore had exploded from the back of Higgins's head as the bullet shattered his skull. What was left of Higgins collapsed on to the crimson covered bed as smoke trailed up from the gun barrel. With the scent of gun smoke in his flared nostrils, the hired killer backed away from the lifeless body on the blood-splattered bed and only turned when he reached the door.

He stepped into the corridor and reached down for the door knob. The tall figure closed the door and then carefully ejected the spent casing from his gun and placed a fresh bullet into the empty chamber. With smoke still trailing from its hot barrel, Danvers holstered the weapon and then made his way to the stairs.

The sound of the gunman's spurs trailed behind him as he slowly made his way back down toward the lobby. Danvers strode across to the desk and paused from a moment as his eyes burned into the seated clerk.

Another cruel smile etched Danvers's face as he touched the brim of his Stetson.

'Remember, friend,' he warned. 'You didn't see or hear a damn thing. Savvy?'

The clerk duly nodded. He watched the gunman slowly walk back to the door and open it. Dust blew in for the brief seconds that the door was open. The clerk could not move from where he sat as he watched the stranger pull his reins free of the hitching pole through the door glass.

Danvers reached up to his saddle horn.

He rose up and swung his right leg across his horse before sitting down upon the saddle. He turned the grey mare away from the hotel and then saw a man fighting against the sand storm. The sand chewing figure had a tin star pinned to his vest and a twin barrelled scattergun gripped across his middle.

The lawman stopped and spat the sand from his mouth.

'Hold on there a minute, stranger,' he shouted against the constant howling of the sand storm. 'Did you have anything to do with that shot I just heard?'

Silently, Danvers held his mount in check with his left hand as the fingers of his right hovered just above his holstered gun. He allowed the horse to move toward the lawman.

The sheriff dragged back on the hammers of his twin-barrelled scattergun and he stood directly in front of the horse. 'Answer me, stranger. Do you know anything about that shot?'

Danvers inhaled as his eyes focused on the tin star.

'I know that Charlie Higgins is dead up in room twelve of the hotel, Sheriff,' he hissed like a sidewinder.

The lawman turned the shotgun on Danvers. 'And just how do you know that?'

Danvers glared down from his high-shouldered horse at the lawman blocking his route out of town. He gave a nod of his head.

'I know that because I killed his sorrowful fat carcass, Sheriff,' Danvers answered dryly. 'Satisfied?'

The shocked expression on the face of the stunned lawman stared blankly up at the horseman who loomed over him. He could not believe that a killer would so freely admit his guilt.

'You done what?' the sheriff gasped at the haunting figure sat astride his grey.

'I killed him,' Holt Danvers repeated as he inched the grey mare closer to the lawman. 'I killed Charlie Higgins with one shot.'

'Why?'

Danvers spat across the distance between himself and the lawman. He stared into the befuddled face of the sheriff and then grinned.

'Hell, I was paid to kill the fat bastard,' he said as the storm grew stronger. 'Nothing personal. Stand aside and I'll be on my way.'

Totally astounded by the statement, the sheriff blinked as storm dust bit into his face. He tilted his head and looked at the devilish horseman.

'If you're telling me the truth, you'd best raise them hands and get ready for the gallows, friend,' the lawman said as his finger stroked his triggers. 'We take killing mighty seriously around these parts.'

'Killing is a mighty serious profession,' Danvers said through gritted teeth. 'So is dying. Now get out of my way or I'll prove it to you.'

'Am I supposed to be frightened by you, boy?' the sheriff asked as he nursed the scattergun in his hands. 'Raise them hands or get ready to die.'

Danvers gave a muted chuckle and then drew his still smoking Peacemaker from its holster at incredible speed. The .45 was cocked, levelled and fired in less time than most men could blink.

The brief flash and ear-splitting shaft of white hot venom caught the sheriff totally by surprise. The lawman felt the impact of the bullet as it hit him. He went to pull back on his triggers.

Once again he was too slow.

Danvers fired again. This time with lethal accuracy.

The flash and deafening explosion echoed around the street. It was the last thing the sheriff would ever witness as he felt the bullet carve into him.

The lawman fell backwards. The hefty scattergun landed beside his dead body as Danvers stared down at his handiwork and laughed out loud.

'Give my regards to Hell, Sheriff,' he muttered before tapping his razor-sharp spurs into the flanks of the mare.

The grey mare walked over the lifeless lawman as its master carefully extracted the spent casings from his gun and swiftly replaced them with fresh bullets from his belt.

The ruthless gunman spat down at the body, holstered his gun and then screwed up his eyes against the biting sand that tormented his scarred features.

Unlike most riders, Danvers did not shy away from the storm that was battering the borderland. He aimed his mount straight toward it and then drove his spurs hard into the flesh of his grey mare.

The tall animal thundered away from the remote settlement at breakneck speed. Danvers was on his way to where he knew his expertise would soon be hired again.

Before the echoing of the lethal shots had ceased resonating, Danvers was gone. Only his bloody handiwork would remain as evidence that he had ever been there at all.

SIX

The black hands of the town clock had not had time to reach two in the afternoon when the storm battered Silver Creek echoed to another familiar noise. It was the sound of an approaching team of sturdy horses drawing their cargo into the remote border town. The driver of the high sided vehicle guided his six horses skilfully around the body of the lawman and on toward the depot.

The stagecoach rattled to a halt as its driver pressed down upon the brake pole with his right boot and jerked the hefty reins to his chest. Clouds of choking dust kept on travelling as the six-horse team snorted outside the stage depot. A tall lean man stepped out from the office and greeted the driver as he checked his clip board.

'You're two hours late, Buck,' the depot

manager noted.

'You try driving in a damn sand storm, Jeb,' the driver answered as he looked over the top of the coach back along the street at the dead lawman's body. 'Who got themselves shot?'

'Sheriff Gibbs,' the depot manager replied without looking to where the body still lay. 'Nobody liked the bastard anyway.'

'He was a pain in the backside.' The driver chuckled. 'Reckon he stepped on the wrong toes once too often.'

Just then the two passengers disembarked from the coach and waited as the driver tossed their saddle bags down into their awaiting arms. The tall men looked nothing like most of the folks who travelled on the stagecoach. They looked danger-ous.

'Who got shot?' one of them asked.

'Just the sheriff.' The driver laughed.

Both men looked at one another.

'At least it cheered someone up,' one of the men said.

The depot manager looked up from his clip board. 'Bobby Fuller the clerk at the hotel said it was a varmint named Holt Danvers that done the killings.'

'Killings?'

The manager nodded. 'Indeed. Danvers killed a fat man in the hotel by all accounts as well. Reckon the sheriff got in the way when Danvers was about to ride on out.'

The stagecoach passengers glanced at each other. Neither man looked like federal officers but that was exactly what they were. They had been sent all the way from Virginia to eliminate the notorious Danvers, who was becoming an embarrassment to the powers that be.

'Danvers again,' one of the men stated.

Jeb Foster and Lane Chandler slung their bags over their broad shoulders and stepped into the shade of the depot porch. The sand storm was easing.

Both Chandler and Foster eyed the long winding street and then glanced at one another. They had been sent by the authorities to put an end to the depraved killer who had roamed freely across the long unmarked border, leaving a string of bodies in his wake.

'It looks like he's added another notch to his gun grip, Lane,' Foster said as his eyes stared through the swirling sand at the lifeless corpse.

'If it's the same critter.' Chandler sighed.

'It has to be.'

Although the law refused to acknowledge the

fact that it had sent its finest agents to kill the noto-rious hired gunman known as Holt Danvers, that was what it had done.

'How far is it to the border, Lane?' Foster asked as he scratched a match down the porch upright and held it to the small black cigar between his lips.

Chandler dried his sweating features with the tails of his bandanna and sighed heavily. His eyes glanced at his partner as he searched for a livery stable.

'I'm told it's five miles as the crow flies,' he answered.

Foster nodded and sucked in smoke. 'Let's go get us a couple of saddle horses and head on out. The sooner we do this, the sooner we can head on back.'

Chandler nodded and moved back into the blistering sun.

'You're right.' He grinned as they both made their way around the tail of the stagecoach. 'This part of the country is just too damn hot. I wanna get this job finished as quickly as we can and then head on back to civilization.'

Although they looked nothing like lethal killers, that was exactly what they were. The only difference between the men they sought and themselves was that they were paid handsomely by the government. They did what the law was unable to do with impunity. They killed the killers who were embarrassing the government.

The sense of relief which greeted them as they walked into the livery stable shade was welcome. They stopped a few yards from a muscular man who was obviously the blacksmith and waited for him to notice their arrival.

Griff Sloane had worked as a blacksmith since he was big enough to wrestle even the strongest of horses into submission. His square jaw jutted at the two strangers who stood close to the glowing forge.

'What can I do for you, boys?' he asked before walking toward them. Although both Foster and Chandler were close to six feet in height they looked quite short by comparison to the burly Sloane.

'Have you got any saddle horses?' Chandler asked as he shied away from the heat of the forge and mopped his face again with the bandanna tails.

Sloane glanced at them. His eyebrows rose to his furrowed temple. It was clear by their appearance that the pair of government agents had travelled a long way in a dusty stagecoach before finding their way to his livery.

'You're looking for horses?' he asked. 'I'd have thought that you'd be looking for a hotel room and a hot bath.'

Foster stepped closer to the large figure. His expression hardened as he eyed the blacksmith up and down.

'Answer the question, big man,' he growled. 'Have you got any saddle horses or not?'

Griff Sloane was not easily intimidated but there was something about these strangers which alerted his senses. He shrugged and stepped back before speaking.

'We got plenty of horses,' he informed the men as his eyes noted their holstered guns. 'You wanna rent or buy?'

'We wanna buy two horses,' Chandler replied. 'We're headed south and there ain't no guarantee that we'll be able to bring the critters back.'

'South?' Sloane repeated. 'You *hombres* headed into Mexico?'

'Yep, we sure are.' Foster nodded and then tossed his cigar on to the hot coals. 'We got business down there.'

Sloane led the pair to a string of horses in the stalls at the rear of the livery stable. He stopped and gestured at the horses.

'Take your pick,' the large blacksmith said.

'Every single one of this bunch has got stamina.'

Foster looked at the horses. 'They look OK. Cut two out and saddle them up.'

Sloane sighed and looked at Chandler. 'Ain't too friendly, is he?'

Chandler looked at his partner. 'He's right, Jeb. You ain't too friendly.'

'My bones hurt too much to be cheerful.' Foster marched back to the sun-drenched stable doors and rested in the merciless rays.

As Sloane prepared the two mounts he watched both men carefully. He could tell they were dangerous just by looking at them. As he threw a blanket on the back of the closest horse, he looked at Chandler.

'You boys talk real funny,' he said as he patted the blanket down until it moulded to the shape of the horse's back. 'I ain't never heard anybody sound like you two varmints. Where you from?'

'Back East,' Chandler answered as Foster glanced over his shoulder at his partner.

'We're from Virginia.'

Sloane picked a saddle up in his bulging arms and threw it on to the horse. As he bent over and drew the cinch strap toward him he looked at Chandler again.

'I've heard of Virginia,' he said. 'I ain't got no

idea where it is, but I've heard of it.'

Foster watched the blacksmith tighten the cinch and then straighten up.

'It snows there,' he commented.

Sloane paused for a moment. His pained look expressed his confusion. 'What the hell is snow?'

'Snow is real white and real cold. Reckon you don't get a lot of it in these parts.'

Sloane shook his head. 'You're joshing with me, ain't you? There ain't no such thing. I ain't stupid.'

Foster watched as a fresh team of six horses were backed up and then secured to the stagecoach before its driver and guard climbed back up on to their high perch. As the driver cracked his long leathers across the backs of the team, the stagecoach continued on its way. He turned and watched as Sloane dropped the fender of the second horse and moved between the two animals.

'That'll be sixty bucks for the nags and forty for the saddles, boys.' He grinned as his powerful hands held the horses in check.

Foster dipped his fingers into his vest pocket and then walked toward the liveryman. He dropped the coins into the palm of Sloane's left hand.

'Two golden eagles,' he said.

The blacksmith looked at the coins and then tested them with his teeth before handing the reins to the two strangers.

'They seem real enough,' he said. 'I ain't never had me no golden eagles before. Most folks around these parts pay with paper money.'

'We only ever pay with coin.' Foster placed his saddle bags just behind the cantle and then secured them with the leather laces attached to the padded cantle.

'Why'd you boys wanna go south?' Sloane persisted as he slipped the coins into his leather apron. 'There ain't nothing down there except grief.'

'Business.' Chandler threw his bags over the neck of his mount and stepped into the stirrup. He grabbed the saddle horn and pulled himself up and onto the horse. 'We've got business down there.'

Griff Sloane eyed both strangers. 'You bounty hunters?'

'Nope,' Chandler replied. 'We're just looking for someone that's bin doing more than his fair share of killing in these parts.'

'Who would that be?' Sloane pressed.

'A hired gunman named Holt Danvers,' Foster responded.

'Looking to help him or stop him?' The blacksmith raised his eyebrows and grinned at the agents.

60

'Stop him,' Chandler said. 'By whatever means it takes.'

Sloane nodded. 'That means killing him. There ain't no other way to handle a paid killer. They gotta be stopped permanent, if you get my drift.'

Chandler eyed the blacksmith. 'What towns lie south of here, friend?'

'Diablo.' The blacksmith watched silently as Foster also mounted his horse and gathered up his long leathers. 'Be careful if you're intending heading there.'

Foster stared at Sloane curiously.

'We're always careful, friend,' he spat.

'I sure hope so.' Sloane turned his back on them and moved to the forge. He reached up and grabbed a long wooden handle and started to pump. The contained coals glowed feverishly as air was forced into them. 'They don't take prisoners down there but they do kill a whole lotta gringos.'

Chandler looked at Foster and shrugged.

'We ain't scared.'

Sloane scratched his head. 'I sure would be. There ain't no law down there.'

'There ain't none here either, is there?' Foster noted as he pointed at the dead lawman still stretched out in the street.

Sloane tapped his nose. 'The difference is that we ain't never needed any law in Silver Creek. Where you're headed is a whole different kettle of fish.'

Both riders steered the horses from the livery into the sunlight. The sand had stopped battering Silver Creek but like them, the storm seemed to be heading south.

They trotted into the dust left in the wake of the stagecoach and then spurred. The government agents headed in exactly the same direction that Holt Danvers had taken after his brief killing spree.

Their mounts gathered pace as they chased the storm. The large blacksmith watched them until they were out of view and then turned around and walked back to his forge. He sat down on the edge of the hot coals and scratched his jaw.

'Those boys are either brave or they're plumb loco,' he muttered before coming to the conclusion that they had to be stupid. Only a fool would dare ride south into the lawless land ruled by outlaws and bandits. 'Plumb loco.'

Their fresh horses fought feverishly against their new owners as both horsemen rode after the man they had been sent West to kill.

Neither Foster nor Chandler knew it but they

were on a route which would take them into the most dangerous place either of them had ever been and it was known as Diablo.

SEVEN

There was a lingering smell that hung over the lawless town of Diablo. Some said it was the fact that they needed to toss fresh lime into the numerous out-houses but a few suspected that there was another reason for the strange odour. Some said that it was the acrid scent of death which lingered in the air as countless bodies rotted in and around the sprawling settlement.

Whatever the truth, it stank.

The sky had turned a vivid crimson as the grey mare came over the dusty rise and was reined in. Holt Danvers stared down upon the town which rested in the twilight world of a place where his breed of man could rest assured that they were safe from both the Mexican and American authorities.

Diablo had grown quickly when it became

obvious that a simple mapping error had created a safe haven for the lawless. For Diablo did not actually exist on the official maps of either country. In fact, a tract of land more than fifty miles long could not be claimed by anyone.

Latin bandits and American outlaws mingled together and gathered within its unmarked boundaries to enjoy the fruits of their illicit labour without ever having to trouble themselves that unwanted lawmen with tin stars might come to dish out justice. Diablo was safe from star packers but far more dangerous in every other way.

The death rate in a town where the only law was gun law tended to be a lot higher than most places. You could die for the simplest of reasons in Diablo. Maybe that was why the air was ripe with the sickening scent of death.

Allowing his grey mare a brief respite about two miles away from the sprawling Diablo, Holt Danvers sat astride his mount and stared at the town which most men would never dare approach. Yet he knew that was where his paymasters were. The men who had willingly paid his fee knowing that he would kill anyone they wished dead.

Danvers scratched a match along his saddle horn and cupped the flickering flame to the tip of his cigar. Smoke drifted from his mouth as his unblinking eyes concentrated on the large town below his lathered up mount.

He blew a long line of smoke at the match and tossed its blackened ember at the ground as he thought about the man who had hired his deadly services. Joe Barnaby was down there somewhere, Danvers thought as he savoured the strong flavour of his cigar.

Barnaby was a man who would not look out of place in any civilized town or city. He looked more like a bank manager than what he actually was. For Barnaby had become wealthy by obtaining land by whatever means available to him.

He had never troubled himself when his offers were rejected by those who knew that they were being taken for a ride. His jovial smile would remain intact on his rotund face as he planned another course of action. For men who lived by their own set of rules always got what they desired. No matter what it was.

Barnaby looked like a gentle soul and yet he was just as dangerous as the men he hired to do his killing for him.

Holt Danvers tapped the ash from his long slim cigar as the street lights began to get themselves lit in the heart of Diablo. Within a few minutes it seemed that the entire settlement was glowing like a fire-flies' convention.

The sun had another hour or so left before it would succumb to the inevitable coming of night but Diablo refused to knuckle down to nature. The town was renowned for never sleeping. Men wanted to drink, womanize and gamble and refused to let nature prevent them.

Yet the men who resisted sleep in order to fuel their vices became even more dangerous and unpredictable as the rot-gut liquor took its toll on their weary bodies and minds. They would start shooting for the slightest of reasons.

Danvers was all too aware that it was not safe to close your eyes in Diablo. Death came swiftly to those who relaxed too long within its confines.

The horseman pulled his pocket watch from his vest pocket and flicked its golden lid open. The scarlet rays of the setting sun illuminated the face of the handsome time-piece.

'Now where would old Barnaby be at this hour?' he asked himself as he returned the watch to the safety of his pocket and gathered up his reins once more. 'Reckon he oughta be in the Buckhorn saloon just about now.'

The thought of getting his hands on the bonus money Barnaby had promised him spurred him on even though he knew that the fat older man could never be trusted. Barnaby had a habit of hiring young drifters to try and kill his hired gunmen to save himself paying the full amount he had agreed.

It was a clever ploy. If the young guns killed their chosen target they would be paid a fraction of what Barnaby actually owed. If they failed he did not have to pay them.

No game of chance was more amusing to Barnaby.

The merciless Danvers gripped his cigar between his teeth and drove his blood-stained spurs into the flesh of the tall grey. The stunned animal bolted beneath Danvers and started down the sandy hills toward Diablo as its master leaned back against his cantle. Putrid smoke trailed over his wide shoulders as he mercilessly whipped the shoulders of his exhausted mare.

EIGHT

No amount of training could have prepared government agents Foster and Chandler for the deadly reality which separated the eastern seaboard from the Wild West. Every rule which the two men had lived by back East meant nothing out here amid the cactus and Joshua trees. This was an unholy terrain where death waited for the unwary and the innocent alike. Their saddle horses shied as the scent of death filled their wide nostrils. Foster glared through the eerie shadows and soon became aware why his mount was nervous. Amid the growing darkness he could see the stained sand. Blood had been spilled in the canyon they were approaching.

'Look, Lane,' the intrepid agent said as he pointed a finger at something ahead of them.

Their horses made their way down the sandy slope to the floor of the canyon.

They steered their saddle horses across the dunes and rode deeper into the high-sided corridor of moonlit rocks. The shadows ahead of them cut across the sand as though painted by some unknown artist yet even the blackness could not conceal the wreckage both horsemen had spotted from high above. They drove their spurs into the nervous horses and pressed on toward the broken debris.

'What do you figure that is, Jeb?' Chandler asked as the sound of their horses' hoofs echoed off the surrounding rocks.

'I ain't sure but it sure smells like death to me,' Foster answered without taking his eyes off the broken prairie schooner.

Both government agents knew that this was a land where the law meant nothing to those who frequented its vast untamed vistas. This was a place where there was only one true law and that was the law of the gun. Those who were fastest on the draw always came out on top. Foster and Chandler intended to redress that imbalance but both men knew that it was not going to be an easy job.

For the law only works when folks want its protection. So far they had not encountered anyone who seemed remotely interested in changing things.

Foster pulled back on his long leathers and stopped his mount as Chandler stopped his own mount beside him. They looked up at the jagged rocks to both sides. Even the coming of night did not reduce the danger the canyon posed.

Foster pointed. 'What do you reckon that is, Lane?'

Chandler steadied his skittish mount and squinted to where his partner was aiming a gloved hand.

'It sure smells like something died over there and has started to rot, Jeb,' he said as he stood in his stirrups and looked all around them at the moonlit rocks which towered above them. 'Something got bushwhacked in this canyon and for all we know the critter is still up in them rocks figuring to add to his tally.'

'You might be right about this being an ambush.' Foster nodded as he too looked all around them. If anything was hiding in the rocks, he knew that they were helpless against him. 'Keep your eyes peeled in case the varmint starts taking target practice again.'

Foster drew one of his holstered weapons and chewed on his lower lip. He glanced across at his pal and then gave a nod of his head.

'Let's go take us a look,' he suggested.

'Lead the way, Jeb,' Chandler said as he pulled his six-shooter from its holster and rested the weapon on his saddle horn as his fingers curled around its grip and trigger. 'Whatever that is, it sure don't look right sitting in the middle of the canyon like that.'

As the horses slowly began to walk forward, Chandler kept looking to his left and right in case the culprit of this crime was still lurking in the rocks.

The air was cooling rapidly as both horsemen steered their mounts toward the large obstacle. With every stride of the mounts it seemed to be getting darker as shadows filled the high-sided canyon. The glowing red sky had faded into a blanket of black velvet. Slowly the countless stars would emerge like precious jewels above the dauntless riders as they closed in on the object of their curiosity.

'What the hell is that, Jeb?' Chandler whispered.

Foster had screwed his eyes up and was squinting as hard as he could but even he could not identify what they were approaching.

'Be careful,' he warned his partner. 'This country has a thousand ways to kill the unwary.'

The pair of saddle horses was brought to a halt twenty feet away from the strange object. Even at this distance the black shadows which had enveloped two thirds of the canyon floor still toyed with the eyes and minds of the horsemen.

'I've got me a notion that's a wagon.' Foster tossed his reins across to Chandler and then slowly rose and looped his leg over the cantle. He rested for a while beside the muscular mount and stared at the object. 'What do you think?'

'If it was a wagon there sure ain't a lot left of it,' Chandler said as he squinted hard into the gloom. 'You might be right though.'

Foster glanced up at Chandler.

'Keep your six-gun aimed at that thing,' he muttered before moving away from the horses. 'I might need cover.'

'Be cautious, Jeb.' Chandler pulled back on his gun hammer until it fully locked and then trained his weapon at the object bathed in shadow. 'I hear they got mountain lions around these parts. Neither of us wanna tangle with one of those critters.'

The thought of there being cougars in the vicinity did nothing to dampen Foster's resolve. He continued to stride into the shadows with his gun pointing ahead of him. The closer he got the more he began to think that he was right. It began to look like something that had once been a wagon before it collided with the unforgiving canyon walls. Foster's eyes darted to every sound as he kept on walking straight toward the object.

'Is it a wagon?' Chandler remained in his saddle, with his primed .45 held in his gloved grip. 'Were you right?'

Foster stepped over what was left of a wheel rim. 'I reckon so, Lane. It sure looks nothing like one now though. It looks like a whole heap of kindling.'

Chandler watched as his partner came to a stop and peered into the belly of the wagon.

'What is it, Jeb?' he asked anxiously.

There were times when words could not describe a situation and this was one of those times. Foster released the hammer of his weapon and then holstered the gun. He turned and looked back at his pal and indicated for Chandler to advance. The mounted agent encouraged his mount forward until it reached the side of his partner.

As Chandler eased back on his reins, he too could see what the strange object was. His head tilted as he slid his gun into its holster.

'What's the matter, Jeb?' he asked his brooding partner.

Foster did not reply.

'You were right. It is a wagon,' Chandler said as he stared down upon the wreckage and torn canvas. 'It's probably bin here for years.'

'I surely doubt that, Lane.' Foster stepped into the belly of the wagon, pulled the flapping canvas aside and stared down upon Frank Carver's dead remains. He knelt, checked the body and then rose back up to his full height.

'How can you tell?' Chandler asked.

'This body is fresh, Lane,' he muttered and stepped over the fractured driver's box before accepting his reins from his partner. 'I reckon it's only bin dead for a few hours at most.'

'Are you sure?' Chandler watched as Foster mounted his horse and eased the horse around.

'Yep. His arms are still flexible, Lane.' Foster chewed on his lip anxiously. 'Rigor mortis ain't set in yet.'

Chandler slowly turned his own horse and eased it alongside his partner. He sighed heavily and looked down at Foster.

'You don't think that this has something to do with the hombre we've come all the way here to capture, do you?' he wondered. 'There must be a hundred killers in these parts, Jeb. Any one of them could have killed this *hombre*.'

Foster nodded.

'Maybe so, Lane. Seems kinda strange that this pitiful critter got himself ambushed by a man who then rode on to Silver Creek though, don't it?'

Chandler looked at the hoof tracks around the area. Even the sand storm had not been able to obliterate them in the confines of the canyon.

'You're right,' he agreed. 'The sand has been churned up but I can see the route taken by the bushwhacker after he'd shot the wagon driver.'

Foster stared at the hoof marks left by Zococa and his burly comrade when they had come across the wreckage. He glanced up at his partner.

'Two other horsemen showed up after the killer rode off and then they headed off in a different direction,' he said thoughtfully as he wondered what lay in the vast desert the riders were headed for. 'Why would anyone ride out there?'

Chandler had dismounted and was checking the interior of the moonlit wagon. He turned and looked at Foster.

'There's blood back here, Jeb,' he announced and pointed at Frank Carver's body. 'And it doesn't belong to that poor critter.'

Foster watched as Chandler climbed back over the tailgate and returned to his mount.

'There was someone else in this wagon?' he

gasped. 'I wonder who?'

'My guess is that it was a child.' Chandler mounted his horse and then leaned toward his fellow agent. 'Those riders must have taken the kid to the mission at San Maria.'

Foster nodded. 'You're right. I'd forgotten that there was a mission in the desert. How do you figure it was a child though, Lane?'

Chandler looked at the sand around their mounts and rubbed his unshaven chin thoughtfully.

'Look at the hoof tracks left by that pair, Jeb,' he said knowingly. 'If one of the horses was carrying a fully grown man or woman, its tracks would be a lot deeper than they are. There ain't any difference in either set of them.'

'That means they found a wounded child.' Foster nodded firmly to himself. 'You're right, Lane. I should have figured that out myself.'

'Don't go fretting, Jeb,' Chandler said as he felt a cold shiver trace his spine. He shuddered and gripped his long leathers firmly in his hands. 'We have to find Holt Danvers and do what has to be done. We can't let ourselves be distracted from the job we've been sent to do.'

'You're right, Lane.' Foster grabbed the saddle horn and swung himself up on to the back of his horse. 'We've bigger fish to fry. We've gotta get hold of this Danvers critter before he kills any other innocent folks.'

Chandler rubbed his neck. 'The big fella at the livery said Danvers was headed south to Diablo. C'mon, we better find this bastard as fast as we can.'

Foster steadied himself, poked his boots into his stirrups and stared through the shadows at the trail south. He knew that he and his fellow government agent were undertaking the most perilous mission of their short lives and yet he was determined that they did what they had been sent to do.

'Do you reckon we've got a chance of succeeding, Lane?' he asked as Chandler drew level with him. 'Danvers is headed into the most lawless place either of us has ever heard about.'

Chandler pulled a tobacco pouch from his vest pocket and then started sprinkling the finely ground makings onto a gummed paper. He licked the paper's gummed edge and then placed it between his lips.

'A whole town full of wanted outlaws and bandits ain't the kind of place to make friends in, Jeb.' He grinned before striking a match with his thumbnail. 'Some might say that we're taking on more than we can chew, but not me.'

'How come?' Foster wondered as his partner filled his lungs with smoke and tossed the match at the blood soaked sand. 'How come you don't think we're taking on more than we can chew?'

Chandler allowed the smoke to filter back out through his teeth before answering his friend. He gave a wry smile.

'By my figuring all we gotta do is start shooting everyone we see in Diablo and eventually we're bound to kill Holt Danvers, ain't we?' He chuckled. 'That is if we don't get shot to ribbons as soon as we ride in there.'

Foster shook his head, stared at the ground before them and nodded. 'Reckon so, Lane. After all, they're all wanted by the law and that means it won't be murder.'

The undeterred horsemen started riding again. They were headed due south. A course which would lead them right into the jaws of death.

Otherwise known as Diablo.

NINE

Both horsemen had made good progress from the mission as they travelled further south toward the infamous Diablo. Unlike the man they were hunting, they arrived in Silver Creek with no intention of killing an unsuspecting victim. As the high-shouldered pinto stallion led the mute Apache out of the darkness into the lantern lit main thoroughfare, they noticed that apart from the solitary saloon, every other one of the stores were shuttered.

The flamboyant Mexican dug his boots into his stirrups and eased back on his long leathers so that Tahoka could draw level with him.

As their mounts walked slowly into the heart of Silver Creek, Zococa glanced at his grim-faced companion. He knew that the massive Apache brave was overflowing with anger at what the mysterious bushwhacker had done to the little female he had discovered amid the wagon debris. Zococa had never seen his friend so hell-bent on making someone pay for their crimes.

The sight of the injured child had affected Tahoka more deeply than anything else had ever done. The large warrior had suffered more brutal wounds than most in his life and yet none of those had hurt him as finding the unconscious Mary had done. The Mexican bandit could tell that his loyal friend was now fuelled by vengeance.

Tahoka would not rest until he snapped the neck of Danvers in his massive hands. That troubled the Mexican bandit, for there was nothing more fearsome than the wrath of an Apache.

They teased their mounts along the street into the street lantern lights. Zococa knew only too well that the mute Tahoka was like a stick of dynamite with its fuse lit when he was riled.

Zococa realized that even he could not control Tahoka when the warrior went on the rampage. There would be fire in his eyes unlike anything anyone could ever imagine. A fire which would only be extinguished by the death of the bushwhacker who had killed the child's father and left her broken and bloodied body for the buzzards.

When they had left the San Maria mission, Mary was still unconscious after having her injuries tended by the monks. Zococa prayed that the tiny child would recover but feared the worst.

'We shall find the villainous Danvers, my little one,' he promised as he saw a flickering glow splashing out from the wide open barn doors of the livery stable. 'Do not trouble yourself. We shall find this evil man and I shall make him pay for what he did to Mary and her father.'

Tahoka shook his head and made a few unmistakable gestures with his huge hands. It was the sign of something being snapped and the famed bandit knew exactly what his partner intended snapping. The Apache did not want Zococa to punish Danvers. He wanted to avenge the crimes himself.

Zococa reached across from his pinto and patted the massive bicep. He realized that it was pointless arguing with the massive warrior.

A solitary street lantern cast its amber light across the street and high-lighted the merciless slaying which had occurred there.

'You can do whatever you want to do with Holt Danvers, Tahoka,' Zococa said as they both spotted the dried pool of blood in the sand before them. Both riders stared down at the stained sand with knowing eyes. They stopped their horses and studied the ground. Then a gruff voice came from within the livery stable to their right.

'It's blood, OK, boys,' it said.

The voice startled both riders. Zococa swung his horse around to face the owner of the deep drawling voice. He steadied the pinto and watched as the muscular blacksmith walked out from the livery stable before being bathed in the street lantern light.

Without even realizing it, Zococa had his fingers curled around the grip of his holstered pistol in readiness as the burly Griff Sloane studied them carefully.

'That's the sheriff's blood,' he informed them. 'A couple of boys from the saloon dragged his carcass off to Ma Smith about an hour ago. She'll box and bury him.'

Zococa moved his mount forward until the high-shouldered animal was within a few feet of the blacksmith. He then rested his hands on his silver saddle horn and looked down upon the large man. It was the first time he had ever encountered anyone nearly as big as Tahoka.

'You do not seem upset by the loss of the sheriff, *amigo*,' he said as the Apache moved his horse beside his own. 'Did you not like the star packer?'

Sloane grinned and shook his head.

'Nobody liked him,' he admitted. 'He was always poking his nose into things that didn't concern him. Nobody likes a bastard like that, do they?'

'We do not get to know many lawmen, *amigo*.' Zococa sighed. 'They are usually chasing us and firing their guns.'

'That's a damn shame.' Sloane chuckled as his eyes darted between the pair of horsemen. 'I reckon the perfect lawman is the kind that drinks coffee and plays checkers all day.'

Zococa was amused. 'I agree with you, *amigo*.'

Tahoka made a few hand signals, which the bandit read before looking back at the blacksmith to translate his friend's question.

'My *amigo* wonders who killed the sheriff, *señor*,' he said. 'I also wonder. Do you have any idea who the killer is?'

Sloane gave a firm nod of his head.

'I sure do,' he said. 'Have you ever heard of a critter named Holt Danvers? He's the hombre that sent Sheriff Gibbs to the happy hunting ground.'

Both horsemen leaned over the manes of their horses.

'We have heard of this gringo, *señor*.' Zococa tilted his head and nodded thoughtfully. 'So he's

the one who killed the lawman? This is very interesting.'

'Interesting? I'd call it damn fatal,' Sloane
answered. 'Danvers killed him sweet. Real sweet
and fast. Then he rode his grey mare over the body
and headed due south. That grey horse sure
pounded Gibbs's face to a pulp.'

The expression on Zococa's face changed to
one of disgust as the blacksmith's words sank in.
He raised his eyebrows.

'It sounds very messy.' He sighed.

Griff Sloane gave out a belly laugh. 'Sure was.
Mind you, the sheriff was never what you'd call
good-looking.'

Zococa glanced at his Apache pal. Tahoka had a
contented grin etched in his scarred features. The
blacksmith had confirmed that they were on the
right trail and that suited the large warrior just
fine.

'Why did Danvers kill the sheriff, *amigo*?' the
bandit asked as he recalled that hired gunmen
usually did not waste bullets on those they had not
been paid to kill. 'I have heard many bad things
about this evil man, but I thought he only killed
those he was paid to kill.'

Sloane gave a slow nod of his head. 'You're right
about him being a paid killer, sonny. He'd already

earned his blood money before Sheriff Gibbs interfered with him.'

'What do you mean, *señor*?'

'Danvers had shot a fat varmint named Charlie Higgins over in the hotel a few minutes before,' Sloane revealed. 'I reckon the sheriff tried to stop Danvers from leaving Silver Creek. A real bad mistake.'

'A very bad mistake, *amigo*,' Zococa agreed.

'A fatal one.' Sloane chuckled.

'It is one that the sheriff will not make again,' the bandit said. 'This I am certain of.'

The blacksmith rested his knuckles on his hips and tilted his head as he studied both horsemen carefully. It did not take too much figuring for the large man to work out who he was talking to. He had heard many tales of the flamboyant Mexican and his silent companion.

'I've heard of you two boys,' Sloane said.

The bandit smiled. 'You have heard of us, *señor*?'

'Sure have. 'A real pretty bandit on a handsome pinto with a big Apache who only talks with his hands. You gotta be Zococa.'

'I am the famous Zococa,' the Mexican bandit corrected and grinned even wider. 'And this is my little elephant Tahoka. We are hunting the killer Holt Danvers.'

Sloane suddenly looked troubled. 'Now that's odd. There were two other men in here a few hours back. They arrived on the stage, bought a couple of my saddle horses and said they were hunting the same critter.'

The smile evaporated from the bandit's face.

'Two others are also hunting Danvers?' Zococa repeated as his mind raced to who could also be hunting the lethal hired gunman. 'Are you sure, *amigo?*'

'Yep.' Sloane rubbed his jaw. 'They were from Virginia back East. They didn't exactly say so but I figured they were government men.'

Zococa looked at the expressionless Tahoka. He then returned his eyes to the large blacksmith bathed in the flickering lantern light.

'Where did they go?'

Sloane raised a hand and pointed south. 'Diablo.'

Zococa fell unusually silent.

The blacksmith moved between the two riders and looked up into the young bandit's troubled face. He gave a shake of his head.

'Them two boys were packing a lot of hardware, son,' he said in a low whisper.

'They looked like they knew how to use their guns. I'd not tangle with them varmints if I were you. It might prove mighty unhealthy considering you boys got bounty on your heads.'

Zococa inhaled deeply and then looked down at the concerned big man. He forced a smile.

'Tahoka and I are not afraid of gringo lawmen, *amigo*,' he said. 'Besides, if the gringos are fancy lawmen they are the ones who should be troubled.'

'How'd you figure that, Zococa?' Sloane asked.

'They are headed to Diablo just like we are.' The bandit shrugged. 'Our kind is welcome in such lawless places but they are star packers. A chicken in a house full of foxes is much safer.'

Sloane gave another laugh.

'You boys want to share my pot of coffee before you continue your ride?' he asked. 'These horses could do with filling their bellies with water from my trough and resting a while. It ain't an easy ride to Diablo even after sundown.'

'This is an excellent idea, *amigo*.' The young Mexican laughed and rubbed his rump. 'I am a little sore.'

Zococa lifted his leg and threw it over the mane of his pinto before sliding to the ground beside the blacksmith. He looked up at Tahoka.

'Tie the horses up to the hitching pole by the trough, little one.' He winked. 'Then come into the livery. We have coffee to drink with an *amigo*.'

There was a low grunt from Tahoka as he dismounted and accepted his partner's long leathers. His hooded eyes watched both men turn and start toward the livery stable.

As Sloane led the flamboyant figure toward the stable, he glanced back at Zococa curiously.

'Why are you two boys after Danvers, Zococa?' he asked the far younger man. 'He ain't the kinda critter I'd wish to tangle with. I can't imagine that you boys are changing professions and becoming bounty hunters. So how come you're after his sorrowful hide?'

'We wish to punish him,' Zococa answered. 'He has done a very bad thing.'

Sloane looked into the bandit's eyes. 'It must be very bad if you two boys are willing to risk your necks in order to right a wrong.'

Zococa removed his sombrero. 'We made a vow, *amigo*. Tahoka wishes to avenge the wrong done to a little girl he found in the wreckage of a bushwhacked wagon. I have never seen the little elephant so angered. She was like a little rag doll when we took her to the mission at San Maria.'

Sloane reached the glowing forge, plucked up his coffee pot and looked back at the handsome bandit. 'Is the little girl dead, Zococa?'

The bandit was quiet for a few heartbeats and then looked up at the massive blacksmith and shrugged.

'I pray that she is not dead, *amigo.*' He sighed as Tahoka lumbered in behind them. Zococa moved closer to the forge and whispered into the blacksmith's ear. 'My little elephant is already angry enough with the bushwhacker Danvers. If he were to find out that the little child has lost her valiant battle I do not think that even the great Zococa could contain him.'

Griff Sloane pulled three tin cups off a shelf, blew the dust from them and placed them on the forge. 'I guess you're tagging along with Tahoka just in case Danvers gets the better of him, huh?'

'*Sí, amigo.*'

'You must be mighty brave to go up against Danvers.'

Zococa watched as the black beverage was poured into the three cups, and then picked up one. He inhaled the fumes and grinned.

'My Tahoka is a very good shot but he likes to use his bare hands to settle his scores,' Zococa said as he handed one of the tin cups to his partner. He watched as the large Apache warrior moved to a corner and rested his aching bones on freshly scattered hay. The bandit turned to Sloane and continued. 'Danvers is not so brave as my little ele-phant. He uses his pistols.'

Griff Sloane looked at the bandit.

'So do you, I'm told.' The blacksmith placed the coffee pot on the coals and blew the steam from his cup.

Zococa smiled.

'*Sí, amigo.* So do I.'

TEN

Even a blind man could have found Diablo. The stench and the constant sound of gunfire drew men from all directions like flies to a dung pile. The infamous town which lay upon a strip of land that did not actually exist was a place which the law had yet to tame into submission.

The sickening aroma drew the most fearsome killers and loathsome creatures into its lawless web. Here, even the most depraved of humanity existed side by side. Diablo had everything which other settlements had with the exception of a sheriff's office.

This was where men like Holt Danvers could boast about their latest horrific crimes with immunity. He rode across the moonlit sand and into Diablo.

The unholy hired killer guided his grey mare into the outskirts of the boisterous settlement and kept jabbing his spurs into his mount's flanks until it reached the centre of the lawless town. Only then did he draw back on his long leathers and allow the exhausted horse to walk as he glared at each and every one of the hundreds of lost souls as they milled around looking for fresh vices to quench their insatiable thirsts.

Danvers caught the scent of stale perfume in his flared nostrils as it overpowered the other less acceptable smells which dominated the wild town. Gun shots echoed all around his high-shouldered grey as the mare steadily proceeded along the hectic street. Danvers paid none of it any notice as he continued on toward the largest and most favoured of the town's saloons. All he could think about was the Buckhorn Saloon and the fat man who had hired his dubious talents.

As the tall grey reached the midway point of the meandering main street, a half dozen men came tumbling out of one of the town's numerous whore houses. Danvers felt his mount spook as the fighting half-dozen men crashed through a hitching rail and rolled across the street toward Danvers. The horse bucked as Danvers fought to keep it under control.

The sound of jaws cracking as clenched fists collided with them filled the night air. Two of the men threw themselves on top of a pair of others and started to kick, punch and bite one another.

Danvers pulled back on his reins and stopped his horse as the men brawled their way from the red brick structure toward him. He steadied the grey as fists kept flying and the men took it in turns to tumble helplessly towards his high vantage point. A man swung his fists and then was lifted off the ground by a well-placed boot. One of the less fortunate men staggered to his feet and went to attack another as his already bloodied face was hit by the barrel of a gun. He staggered backward and smashed through the display window of a store.

Danvers managed to steady his alarmed mare and watched angrily as the fight continued all around him. He narrowed his eyes and stared at the lantern lit brawl as one man took a well-placed blow to his chin and was sent rolling between his horse's legs.

The grey mare reared up as the rest of the men crashed into his horse. One of the group grabbed a much smaller man and hit him so hard teeth could be seen flying heavenward.

The hired assassin swung his horse around and stared down at the men who were wrestling one another. Danvers looked to the open entrance to the brothel and stared at the dozen or more whores who were loudly encouraging the blood covered men to continue their mindless battle.

Danvers gritted his teeth and drew his six-gun from its holster. He waved the .45 at the men but they either did not see the weapon or did not give a damn.

'Quit troubling my horse, you knuckle-brained bastards,' he shouted at them. They continued to exchange blows. One was sent backwards by a back-handed blow. He hit a hitching pole and tumbled over it.

It seemed whatever had started the fight inside the whore house had not only riled the half dozen men, but also caused them to become totally deaf as well.

Danvers cocked his gun hammer as he fought to keep his trail weary mount under control. He aimed the gun at the three men who were still reasonably upright and then fired in quick succession.

Even in the moonlight it was easy to spot the plumes of blood which erupted from the three men he had shot. Each of the trio was lifted off the sand and thrown backwards.

As the others got to their feet in a daze, Danvers cocked and fired his gun over and over again until its smoking chambers were empty. He swung the grey mare full circle and exchanged his empty gun for the fresh one holstered on his left hip.

As the wounded men suddenly realized what was happening, Danvers fired repeatedly until none of them were standing and what life they had once had, was gone.

'That'll teach you bastards,' he growled as the dust settled over the six corpses. He looked in the direction of the brothel. The highly painted females did not appear to be upset by his handiwork as they took a fresh bunch of clients up the staircase into the depths of the brothel.

In any other town the deafening shots would have brought swift interest from the sheriff but not in Diablo. Life was fleeting in the infamous settlement.

Death came easy.

Gunsmoke hung around the lethal horseman as he quickly shook the spent casings from his guns and hastily reloaded. In less than two minutes both guns had been fully replenished and were thrust back into their holsters.

'Damn it all,' Danvers cursed to himself. 'I hate killing for free. There just ain't no profit in killing for free.'

His thoughts returned to those of his current

paymaster Joe Barnaby and the bonus the fat man had promised him. He turned the tired horse and jabbed his spurs. The mare started to continue on its course toward the Buckhorn.

As the grey mare trotted, Danvers looked up from beneath his wide flat hat brim. He noticed that not one of the many people on the street seemed to be interested in either the killer or his latest victims.

'I hate wasting bullets on folks I ain't being paid to kill,' he grumbled again as his mount gathered pace along the brightly lit thoroughfare. In the distance he could see the Buckhorn saloon. The sound of the deafening volley of gun shots had not drawn a solitary look from the crowd wandering close to the drinking hole.

The grim-faced horseman guided his mare to a hotel on the opposite side of the street from the saloon. He eased back on his reins and then slowly dismounted. The tall Danvers led his horse to the closest trough as he carefully observed the many men and women who gave him a wide berth. Smoke still rose from his holstered guns as his weaponry slowly cooled.

Danvers looped his long leathers over a hitching pole and then tied a secure knot in them. His horse dropped its head and started to drink from the trough.

He stepped up on to the creaking boardwalk to gain a better vantage point and then looked around the moonlit town in case any of his latest victims might have avenging kin.

Diablo had never looked quite as busy to the hired gunman as he pulled a cigar from his pocket and bit off its tip. His cold eyes studied every aspect of the streets which surrounded him as he placed the cigar between his teeth and then ran a match down an upright porch. He nestled the flame between his gloved hands and sucked its fire into the long black weed. Smoke trailed from his mouth as he dropped the match into the trough his grey was drinking from.

Diablo was busy as always. The settlement never slept like most lawful places. It saw no difference between day and night and just continued. An eerie glow filled the entire town as Danvers filled his lungs with smoke and watched the familiar and unfamiliar faces going about their rituals.

Lantern light cascaded out from the doors and windows of nearly every structure. Red silk hung outside a third of the buildings and swayed in the nightly breeze. Danvers rested his wrists on his holstered hardware and then turned to study the Buckhorn Saloon directly opposite him. The saloon was as rowdy as usual as men fuelled themselves in readiness for visiting the whore houses. Danvers stared through cigar smoke at the building and toyed with one of his guns.

He knew that Joe Barnaby might be his best client but he was a slippery customer at the best of times. Danvers had been forced to shoot two of Barnaby's hirelings dead the last time he had tried to collect his bonus money from the misshapen man. The middle-aged Barnaby was always trying to get away with not paying his hired gunmen their promised bonus.

It was a game he played. A game which was as dangerous as the hired gunmen he employed. Barnaby was always hiring the unwary newly arrived outlaws to test their metal. So far it had cost the lives of all the men who had tried to outdraw Holt Danvers.

There seemed to be nothing to concern the devilish killer anywhere close to the Buckhorn. If Barnaby was inside the saloon, he was probably alone and in the company of his favourite brand of whiskey.

As a trio of horses passed the tail of his grey on their way to one of the town's many gambling dens, Danvers stepped down from the boardwalk and started toward the saloon. As he strode across the wide street, more horsemen steered their mounts around the tall figure. A trail of smoke hung in the night air from the cigar gripped between the gunman's teeth.

'One day I'll have to kill Barnaby,' Danvers muttered to himself as he considered the annoying ritual he was always forced to play with the rich Barnaby. 'I'm getting mighty tired of his games.'

Reaching the saloon, Danvers paused and looked to both sides before he stepped up on the boardwalk and pushed its doors apart and entered. They swung on their hinges behind the devilish back of the alert Danvers. The saloon was full. So full it was impossible to see the sawdust covered floor he was walking across.

Danvers narrowed his eyes and squinted through the tobacco smoke at every face. He wondered if Barnaby might have hired any new boys in an attempt to save paying out the bonus money he owed the hired killer.

Even though Diablo was lawless and filled to over-flowing with the scum of two nations, it seemed that every one of those within the Buckhorn recognized the danger as Danvers walked between them. They moved out of his way so that he would not draw either of his six-shooters and start killing.

Perhaps this time was going to be different, Danvers silently thought. Maybe this time the fat old man would not try to save himself the money he had promised to pay his lethal henchman.

The table where Barnaby was seated had four hardback chair's surrounding it. Three were filled with dancehall girls in various stages of decay and the fourth somehow managed to support the weight of the large man himself. The smell of the females' stale perfume was overpowering but it masked the aroma of sweat.

Barnaby glanced up at the dust-caked Danvers. A sickly smile filled his face. There was no acknowledgement in his expression.

With smoke billowing from his mouth, Danvers stepped close between two of the females and stared down at Barnaby who was refilling their glasses with the amber liquor. The closest of the females looked at the man standing close to her bare shoulder. She gave a cooing noise and looked at the bulge just below his belt buckle. Her fingers itched to explore the tall gunman. Danvers looked down at the female and shook his head at her before returning his attention to Barnaby.

'It's done, Joe,' he drawled through a cloud of cigar smoke. 'Done and dusted.'

Barnaby looked at Danvers.

'Both of them?' he queried.

'Yep. Both of them.' Danvers nodded as his eyes scanned the many faces which surrounded the table. 'Just like you ordered.'

The fat man rubbed his many chins and downed the glass of whiskey before refilling the thimble glass again.

'Impressive, Holt. Very impressive indeed,' he remarked.

Flattery had never meant anything to Danvers. He removed his gloves and tucked them into his gun belt. 'Now it's time for you to honour your side of the deal, Joe.'

'Honour?' Barnaby chuckled. 'I doubt if any of us know the meaning of that word, Holt. If we did, we'd not be in this stinking town.'

Danvers snapped his fingers and drew the attention of the watery eyes to him and his holstered hardware.

'I'm still waiting for my bonus, Joe,' he snarled.

Suddenly, just as Danvers had finished speaking, he caught the glimpse of a lantern light flashing above him on the staircase to the second floor. Barnaby had done exactly as Danvers had suspected and hired another cheap young outlaw to kill him. The nickel-plated .45 had betrayed its youthful owner and signalled the deadly Danvers that it had been drawn from its holster.

Without a moment's hesitation, Danvers drew both his guns, aimed at the young outlaw on the steps and fired. Both bullets hit the outlaw dead centre. Blood suddenly covered the youngster's shirt front. The impact of the bullets had caused him to buckle as the gun hung on his finger before falling on to the wooden boards. Danvers cocked his hammers again and fired two more shots into the already stricken figure. Every eye within the Buckhorn watched as the man toppled forward and crashed down the staircase. He came to a halt just behind Barnaby's chair.

'Good shooting, Holt,' the fat man said.

Danvers glared at Barnaby. 'How much did you promise that kid, Joe?'

Barnaby shrugged.

'Not as much as I promised to pay you, Holt,' he admitted. 'Oh well, it was worth a try.'

Furiously Danvers shook his head and aimed his guns at the seated man before him. 'I oughta kill you for that. Killing cheap thugs ain't profitable.'

Barnaby looked up at the riled Danvers.

'Your bonus money is in my safe, Holt.' He smiled. 'If you kill me you'll never get your money. Only I know the combination.'

Danvers holstered his guns. He knew the fat

man was correct and he would never see a dime of his payment if he submitted to his anger. He snorted as his eyes burned into the seated Barnaby.

'I reckon you want paying, huh?' the older man grunted and downed his whiskey in one well-rehearsed action.

Danvers gave a silent nod of his head.

'Are you sure you killed them both, Holt?' Barnaby asked as he refilled his glass.

'Yep,' Danvers said. 'Both dead just like that dead kid behind your fat backside.'

Barnaby's watery eyes stared through the tobacco smoke at the hired killer. He raised his head to reveal his fleshy throat.

'Are you telling me that you've killed both of them critters, Holt?' he taunted. 'That's mighty fast work, even for you.'

Danvers pulled the cigar from his mouth. 'You wanted them dead and they're dead. Now pay my bonus or you'll be joining them.'

Barnaby rocked with laughter and slapped the table top with his hands. 'That's what I like about you, Holt. You always make me laugh.'

'I ain't joshing, Joe,' Danvers rasped before sucking the last of the cigar's smoke from the spent weed.

'I know you ain't.' Barnaby chuckled. 'That's what I'm laughing at. You never joke. You take everything so damn seriously.'

With no warning Danvers pushed the females off their chairs and moved closer to the table edge. His narrowed eyes burned at the overweight man seated opposite him.

'Pay up or die, Joe,' he growled before tossing the cigar at one of the females on the ground. 'It's up to you. I'm through making you laugh.'

Barnaby waved his hands in surrender at the snarling Danvers. He knew how far he could push Holt Danvers and he had reached that mark.

'OK, Holt.' He laughed before pushing his chair back and slowly rising. 'No need to get ornery. I'll pay you just like we agreed.'

Danvers straightened up as his paymaster walked unsteadily around the table toward him. Barnaby pulled up his pants and adjusted his derby before curling his finger at the unsmiling gunman.

'Follow me, Holt,' he said as he headed through the crowd for the swing doors. 'Let's go to my office. I'll pay you your damn bonus.'

Both men made their way through the crowded saloon toward the swing doors. Neither trusted the other as far as they could have thrown them but were joined together by some invisible force. No matter how great their mutual loathing, they needed one another.

Danvers trailed Barnaby out into the lantern lit street.

ELEVEN

Foster jerked back on his reins and stared across the moonlit sand to where Diablo glowed like a swarm of fireflies. He raised his left hand and pushed the brim of his hat off his face. The sight of the well-illuminated settlement did not sit well with the government agent as he steadied his mount and saw Chandler stopping his own horse. He looked at the troubled expression on his partner's face before returning his eyes to what lay a few miles ahead of them.

The acrid smell drifted across the moonlit sand and filled their nostrils as they sat astride their weary mounts and rested for a few moments. Chandler patted the neck of his horse and vainly tried to rub the smell from his nose with the back of his glove.

'Sure stinks, Jeb,' he said as his eyes remained fixed upon the lantern light. 'I've never known any town that smells as bad as that one.'

Foster nodded in agreement.

Foster wondered whether they could achieve their goal and then get out of Diablo in one piece. He rubbed his eyes as he stared at the brightly illuminated settlement.

'It's a whole lot bigger than I figured,' he said before unscrewing the stopper of his canteen and taking a mouthful of its warm contents.

Chandler gave a nod of his head. 'It sure is large, Jeb.'

'I never thought that Diablo was that big, Lane.' Foster sounded nervous as he returned his canteen to beside the coiled rope.

'Me neither.' Chandler sighed and then looked to his partner. 'A town that large must be full of outlaws and bandits just like Danvers, Jeb. Most are probably wanted dead or alive and not the kind we wanna bump into.'

'And we gotta ride in there,' Foster repeated their orders. 'Ride in and find Holt Danvers.'

Chandler raised an eyebrow. 'It sure sounds easy if you say it fast enough. The problem is when you dwell on it.'

Both agents checked their arsenal and then

resolved themselves to the job they had been commanded to undertake.

Foster inhaled deeply.

'You ready, partner?' he asked.

'Guess so,' Chandler muttered.

'We should get there in roughly an hour,' Foster said as he slapped his reins and started his horse moving again. 'I reckon it'll be like looking for a needle in a haystack just trying to locate Danvers in a town of that size.'

Chandler nodded as he gathered up his loose leathers.

'I sure hope we find that bastard quickly.' He sighed heavily. 'I don't hanker staying there too long, Jeb. I don't think it'll be too healthy for the likes of us.'

'C'mon, Lane,' Foster urged as he mount started to trot. 'There ain't no point in brooding on this. We've got a job to do so let's do it.'

Chandler tapped his spurs into the flanks of his mount and followed his fellow agent toward Diablo. He did not utter a word as both horsemen closed the distance between the notorious town and themselves.

TWELVE

The Mexican bandit and his giant companion rode quickly toward the infamous Diablo. Both wanted to reach the lawless settlement as fast as possible in order to stop Holt Danvers from adding to his bloody tally. Zococa had led the way astride his pinto stallion since bidding farewell to the sturdy blacksmith and used every shortcut available to them to reach their destination. Those unfamiliar with the uncharted strip of land that the lawless breed of men had occupied for nearly a decade were totally unaware that you could reduce the distance between Silver Creek and Diablo by nearly half.

Apart from a blanket of purple sagebrush, the route to and from Diablo was obstacle free. Zococa and Tahoka had used its secluded terrain to avoid many a dogged posse over the years and were more than familiar with it winding trails.

The huge Apache drew level with his partner and stared through the undergrowth at the glowing amber light ahead of them. His hooded eyes focused on the moonlit settlement as the bandit gave him vital instructions with his free hand. Tahoka nodded and then leaned over the neck of the thundering horse beneath him.

Although they were aware that they were not the only horsemen heading for Diablo intent on getting their hands on Holt Danvers, they didn't know they had already overtaken the pair of government agents as they emerged from a cactus covered gully and whipped their mounts' shoulders. The Mexican bandit and his silent companion rode up a sandy rise and stared straight ahead at the fragrant Diablo.

They did not waste a solitary second thinking about what might face them when they eventually reached their goal. They just drove their horses on through the darkness.

Had either of them glanced to their right, they might have spotted the pair of law officers making their own way toward Diablo but all thoughts were focused on only one thing. They could not think of anything except reaching the remote town and finding the merciless man known as Holt Danvers.

Within a mere heartbeat they had reached the outskirts of the town and drew back on their long leathers. Both horses slowed to a walk as they entered the sprawling array of structures from its eastern corner.

There were rags fluttering in the moonlight from broken window frames above and below the crudely painted sign, which hung from the fragile remnants of the porch overhang. Their weathered fabric gave no clue that they had once been colourful drapes. This was the one part of Diablo where even the hardest of its inhabitants seldom ventured.

This was where the dregs of its unruly citizens ended up when even their dubious talents were no longer valued or needed by the paymasters who controlled everything within the boundaries of Diablo. Those who had fallen from grace and were no longer trusted to do what had placed bounties upon their heads. Diablo was a tough place to exist if you could not muster the skills which had brought you to this safe haven.

Both Zococa and Tahoka noticed that this part of Diablo was strangely dark by comparison to the rest of the devilish town. Men moved in and out of shadows around the neglected structures like lost souls.

They no longer lived but simply existed. Bitter by the lot they had brought to themselves. Some might have said that they were burdened by guilt for the things they had done in the past whilst others saw it for what it actually was.

When men play too hard and drink anything they can get their hands upon, they have simply resigned themselves to the inevitable. The Mexican bandit knew that they were still a half mile from the very centre of town but he needed to allow their mounts to rest and drink.

He waved a hand and pointed at a trough. Tahoka nodded.

Both horsemen turned the heads of their horses toward the creaking remnant of what had once been an impressive building but was now a structure ready to collapse.

Darkness veiled the wooden structure as the exhausted horses neared its long water troughs. Zococa leaned against his cantle and studied the building carefully. To have ever called it a saloon would have been to insult the intelligence of those who frequented the solitary structure yet that was what it proclaimed to be.

A weathered sign with the word painted across its worm-eaten façade rocked on its rusty chains from the porch overhang. The light from many candles and oil lamps spilled out from within the heart of the saloon.

The outline of the ramshackle building was high-lighted by the moonlight which managed to penetrate this part of Diablo and yet not even the shadows could hide the reality from the mute Apache or his companion's knowing eyes.

'This is not the most appealing of cantinas, my little one,' Zococa announced as he stopped the stallion. 'But our horses are thirsty and so am I.'

Tahoka glanced at his exuberant cohort and made urgent hand signals which Zococa dismissed with a grin.

'I know we came here to teach Señor Danvers a lesson, Tahoka.' He shrugged. 'But the horses are thirsty and so am I, little one. Besides, we do not know where he is. Diablo is a big town and there are many drunken men inside the saloon who could inform us where to find him.'

The brave was still not happy at Zococa going into the saloon. Yet none of his objections were taken seriously by the confident bandit.

'You worry too much, little one.' Zococa sighed before looping his leg over the neck and head of the pinto and sliding from its saddle. Dust rose up into the night air as his boots landed on the ground. Tahoka shook his head as they both looked at the uninviting structure before them.

Zococa tied his reins to the hitching pole and allowed his mount to continue drinking from the trough. He pulled his nickel-plated pistol from his holster and checked that it was fully loaded. He then slid the weapon back into its hand-tooled home and looked back at the burly Apache.

'I think that you should remain outside, *amigo*,' the bandit suggested as the sound from within the decayed structure grew louder. 'The *hombres* might not greet me with the respect I deserve.'

Tahoka dismounted and hastily tied his reins to the hitching pole. He then slid his carbine from its saddle scabbard and pushed its hand guard down. A spent casing flew from its magazine before he returned the guard back to its normal position.

Zococa was known on both sides of the border for his daring deeds and matchless skill with his nickel-plated pistol but even he needed the support of his faithful friend when entering unfamiliar places such as this.

He stepped on the bottom rung of the boardwalk steps and quickly moved up through the shadows until the light from within the interior of the saloon cascaded over him. Zococa hesitated for a moment as the lumbering Apache warrior ascended to his side.

'Stay here and watch, *amigo*.' Zococa smiled before placing his hand on the top of the swing doors, pushing them apart and entering.

Although the famed bandit had faced many heavily armed men before, there was something different about the crowd which filled the saloon. They were well-armed with a variety of weapons and well-liquored but there seemed to be something else which Zococa sensed.

Every one of them watched as Zococa walked across the sawdust-covered floor boards toward the bar counter. As he reached his destination he had counted more than twenty men within the nameless drinking hole. Every one of them shared a similar trait and that was that they looked as though they were ready to draw their guns and start killing at any moment.

The bandit sensed that his arrival had caused more than a sense of curiosity among the occupants of the bar room. It had caused their hostility to rise from the depths of their mutual despair and focus that anger in his direction.

Zococa pushed the brim of his sombrero off his temple to rest on the crown of his head. He looked at every face that was staring in his direction and knew what they were thinking.

'What'll it be, friend?' the bartender asked.

116

'Tequila, *amigo*,' he answered as he rested a hip against the bar counter and kept observing the crowd of watchful patrons. Most were seated at circular tables dotted around the bar room but a few leaned on the counter at the far end of the saloon.

The bandit produced his silver cigar case and flicked it open. The dent caused by the bullet which had tried to kill Zococa made the operation slower than usual. The handsome bandit pulled a cigar from the case and placed it between his teeth. He then struck a match and cupped its flame to the tip of his cigar.

The bartender placed the glass of tequila down next to the bandit and accepted the silver coin Zococa dropped into the palm of his hand.

'Anything else?' the bartender reluctantly asked.

Zococa smiled through the smoke that was billowing from his mouth. 'A pretty *señorita* would be nice, *amigo*.'

The bartender grunted and walked to where the rest of his hard drinking customers were gathered. 'Not even the dumbest of females ever come to this end of town, boy.'

Zococa savoured his cigar as he kept watching the men who glared in his direction. Most men would have made a hasty exit but not the flamboyant young bandit. He just kept grinning and puffing on his cigar. He turned to the gathered crowd within the confines of the saloon.

'I am seeking an hombre called Holt Danvers, *amigos*,' he said with a raised, animated flourish of his right arm. 'Do any of you know of him?'

There was a hushed silence before one of the three men stood along the bar counter moved away from the others and glared at the bandit.

'Who are you, stranger?' he shouted angrily. 'What you doing here? We don't cotton to fancy dressed *hombres* coming in our saloon. You look like a bounty hunter to me. Is that what you are?'

Zococa exhaled a line of smoke at the floor and then picked up his drink and downed it in one swift action. He pushed the glass into the middle of the bar counter and signalled for it to be refilled.

'I am not a bounty hunter, *amigo*.'

Zococa sighed as the bartender walked toward him and poured more tequila into his glass. The lean figure leaned across the counter and warned him in a low whisper. 'I'd drink that and skedaddle if I was you, sonny. The boys in here will surely kill you, if you don't.'

Unconcerned, Zococa puffed on his cigar and tossed another coin at the bartender.

'You should not worry about Zococa, *amigo*.' He

smiled. 'I am probably worth more dead or alive than any of your other customers.'

The bartender shrugged and returned to his noisy patrons and made a vain attempt to quiet them down.

'What did you say your name is, dude?' another of the standing men shouted at the bandit. 'Did you say your name's Zococa?'

His companions all started to chuckle.

Zococa lifted the small glass and took a sip of the clear liquor. He then placed the glass back down as the fingers on his left hand flexed.

'I fail to see what is so amusing, *amigos*,' Zococa stated as his eyes darted between the three men who were trying to get him riled. 'Have you never heard of the great Zococa?'

'I have but you ain't him, dude,' the largest and loudest of the trio grunted. 'Zococa is a real man and you ain't nothing but a little boy.'

The bandit grinned and then dropped his cigar into a spittoon at his feet. 'I am the great Zococa, *amigo*. If you wish I shall prove this to you.'

'How you gonna do that, boy?' the loud man shouted at the calm figure facing him.

'I will draw my pistol and prove it,' Zococa warned. 'The problem is that every time I draw my pistol, gringos tend to die.'

Mike Murphy was older than his two brothers and at least six inches taller. Yet age and height had not bestowed the stagecoach robber with any more brains than his siblings. He did not recognize the fact that death was standing a mere ten feet from where he stood and continued to push his luck.

'My name's Murphy,' he shouted at the smiling bandit. 'Mike Murphy and these are my brothers Moses and Rufus. We're stagecoach robbers and killers. We ain't no pip-squeak who pretends to be a famous bandit.'

Zococa shrugged. 'I have heard of you. You used to be very good at robbing the stagecoaches but I thought you must have been killed because I have not heard about you in many years.'

The face of Mike Murphy went ashen.

'Me and my brothers ain't dead, boy,' the outlaw snarled at Zococa. 'We just decided to hole up here for a while.'

The bartender reached across the counter and tugged on Murphy's shirt sleeve. The eldest of the bothers did not look at the bartender as he growled at him. 'What do you want, Slim?'

'Look at him, Mike,' the bartender urged. 'He's a leftie. A southpaw.'

'So what, Slim?' Murphy yelled at the bartender.

'Lots of folks are lefties.'

The bartender shook his head. 'You don't understand. Zococa is Mexican lingo. It means someone who favours his left hand side, Mike. That young critter is a leftie, just like they say Zococa is.'

Moses moved to his elder brother's side. 'That's right, Mike. Slim's right. That young critter is a leftie just like Zococa. It might be him.'

Mike Murphy shook his head. 'It can't be him, I tell you. He's too damn young, Moses. Zococa gotta be older. He's just gotta be.'

Rufus Murphy might have been the youngest of the brothers but he was not blessed with an ounce more brains. He downed his whiskey and looked between Mike and Moses at the still smiling young bandit.

'I don't reckon he's Zococa,' he drawled. 'He's just a kid trying to get a rise out of you. Don't back down, Mike. Shoot the bastard.'

'Come to think about it, Mike.,' Moses pulled on his brother's sleeve. 'He can't be Zococa. They say that Zococa always travels with a big Injun. Ain't that right?'

'You're right, Rufus.' Mike smiled and nodded as he squared up to Zococa and pushed his jacket over his holstered gun grip. 'Come on, sonny.

Prove to me that you is who you say you is.'

Zococa kept watching the three men as he lifted the glass off the bar counter and calmly drank the tequila. He then placed the glass down and stared at them. The light of candles danced across the Murphy brothers' enraged faces. He turned to face them like a matador confronted by three bulls.

'You may draw first, *amigos*,' he told them as he glanced over their shoulders at the doorway. 'It does not matter to me.'

'He talks real tough for an hombre on his lonesome, Mike,' Moses Murphy grunted as he rested his hand on the wooden grip of his .45.

Zococa looked from beneath the wide brim of his sombrero and smiled broadly at the men who were determined to end his colourful existence.

'I am never alone, *amigos*,' he stated.

At that same exact moment Slim suddenly heard his saloon doors creak. He turned and stared at the massive Apache stood in the flickering lantern and candle light. The bartender gasped and pressed his backbone up against the shelf behind him. Tahoka was like a man mountain as he gripped his rifle across his chest with his finger wrapped around its guarded trigger. The bartender was trying to speak but all he could do was make grunting noises.

The youngest of the Murphy brothers was watching the skinny bartender in amused glee. Terror had the lean Slim by the throat. Rufus snapped his fingers in an attempt to get the man's attention.

'What's wrong with you, Slim?' Rufus Murphy laughed at the sight of the terrified bartender. 'You look like you done seen a ghost or something.'

Finally the bartender managed to splutter words from his trembling mouth. 'Look behind you, for heaven's sake. Look behind you while you still can.'

No sooner had the words of warning tripped from the bartender's lips when the seated patrons of the dilapidated saloon also noticed its newest arrival.

A mutual gasp went around the saloon as the watchful audience also noticed the huge figure. Suddenly Tahoka cranked the mechanism of his carbine. The distinctive sound went around the bar room.

Mike Murphy's eyes widened. 'What was that?'

His brother Moses turned his head and inhaled quickly.

'Holy cow!' he gasped in startled amazement. 'You'd best take a look at what just blew in, Mike.'

Mike Murphy's unblinking eyes flashed between Zococa and his brother. 'What you babbling about, Moses?'

'This young Mexican must be Zococa, Mike.' Moses gulped as he rubbed the sweat off his whiskered face. 'Look at the size of that Injun.'

Zococa watched as the eldest of the brothers looked over his shoulder at Tahoka before returning his snarling features to stare at him.

'I ain't feared of no Apache.' The stagecoach robber spat at the ground. 'No matter how big the galoot is. We'll just have to kill him as well.'

Rufus gulped as well. 'If we got bullets big enough.'

Moses shook his head and gripped the wooden bar counter.

'I don't wanna die tonight, Mike,' he pleaded with his brother. 'Quit this and settle down before we're all having pennies placed on our eyeballs.'

Mike Murphy had drunk too much whiskey to consider his options rationally. He was in no mood to back down from the handsome bandit or his gigantic companion. He shook his head and glared at the Mexican bandit.

'I'm gonna wipe that smile off that bastard's face, Moses,' he growled. 'You can back up my play or high-tail it like snivelling cowards. I don't give a damn. I'm killing him.'

Moses and Rufus looked at each other and then to both sides of their brother. They were torn between leaving their determined sibling to face both Zococa and the giant Tahoka on his lonesome or saving their own bacon and running for cover. Neither choice seemed right to the drunken outlaws but blood was thicker than water. Both shrugged and pushed their coat tails over their holstered gun grips.

'Hell. We can't leave you to face these critters alone, Mike,' Rufus said as he turned and stared at the giant Apache warrior while his older siblings faced Zococa.

Moses pushed himself away from the bar and stood beside his older brother, facing Zococa.

'This has gotta be the dumbest thing you've ever got me tangled up in,' he snorted. 'If that is Zococa, we're dead meat.'

Zococa shook his head. 'You are making a big mistake, *amigos*. We do not wish to kill you. We only want to know where Holt Danvers is.'

'Danvers ain't no better than a stinking bounty hunter,' the eldest of the Murphy brothers spat in contempt. 'A low-life, scum sucking bounty hunter.'

'This is true, *señor*,' Zococa agreed before adding, 'my little friend over there and I were saving our ammunition to kill him.'

The bar room rocked as Mike Murphy suddenly

yelled, crouched and went for his gun. Within a mere split second all three of the brothers had managed to drag their weaponry from their holsters and were about to fan their gun hammers.

Zococa drew his pistol faster than either of the men who faced him had ever witnessed anyone pull a gun from a holster before. With an expertise that defied the eyes of the saloon's onlookers, his first three bullets had hit their targets and sent both Moses and Mike Murphy spinning on their boot leather as blood sprayed out from their horrific wounds.

Rufus was about to start shooting at the Apache when he heard the muffled moans of his brothers before both men fell to either side of him.

His eyes stared down in disbelief at his dead and dying siblings for a few moments before he snarled at Tahoka.

'Die, you bastard,' Rufus screamed as he fanned his gun hammer and fired wildly at the massive Indian. His bullet might have come close had he not been so hysterical. A chunk of wood was splintered off the door frame as Tahoka simply squeezed his Winchester's trigger.

There was a sickening groan from the youngest of the brothers. His six-shooter fell from his hand as blood began to spread across his shirt front.

Rufus Murphy staggered and stared in disbelief at his chest and then shook his head and looked at the massive warrior.

'Damn it all,' he mumbled as blood trailed from his mouth. 'You done killed me, Injun.'

His eyes rolled up into his head and he fell between his outstretched brothers. Within seconds the meagre sawdust scattered on the floor was covered in red gore. Tahoka walked quietly across the saloon and cast his hooded eyes on the dead men. Zococa stepped carefully over the bodies and patted his companion on the shoulder.

'Bravo, little one,' he said before looking at the terrified bartender and curling his finger. 'A bottle of whiskey for my *amigo*, Señor Slim.'

The shaking bartender picked up a whiskey bottle and placed it before Tahoka.

'On the house.' He nodded to the expressionless Apache warrior before turning to Zococa as the young bandit carefully replaced spent shells with fresh bullets from his belt. 'You asked where Holt Danvers is, Zococa.'

The bandit glanced at the bartender.

He nodded and slid his pistol back into its hand-tooled holster. '*Sí, amigo*. My little elephant and I are looking for the evil creature called Holt Danvers. Do you know where we can find him?'

'The Buckhorn saloon,' the bartender replied. 'It's the biggest saloon in Diablo and situated in the middle of town.'

'*Gracias, amigo.*'

THIRTEEN

Jeb Foster had eased back on his reins as he and his partner reached the edge of the vast town. Chandler trotted alongside his friend's saddle horse and stared into the brightly illuminated town. Diablo looked no safer, whichever route you chose to enter it by. The streets were still full to overflowing with more traffic than most other settlements could muster during the day, let alone the night.

Chandler looked to both sides of the street as they continued along the winding street on course to the very heart of Diablo. Like his partner he had never seen so many saloons, gambling halls or brothels in such close proximity before.

'We'd better pray that none of the outlaws we've arrested in the past recognizes us, Jeb,' he said as he pulled the brim of his Stetson down over his brow. 'If we do get spotted I reckon every damn gun within this town will be aimed in our direction.'

Foster sighed heavily as they noticed the pile of dead bodies strewn across the sand before them. They steered their horses carefully around the corpses and continued on.

'That looks like the work of the varmint we're after, Lane,' the government agent remarked. 'He tends to kill and just leave his victims to rot.'

Chandler shook his head. 'This town is full of similar gunmen just like Danvers, Jeb. I don't reckon he killed them *hombres*.'

Foster guided his horse close to the boardwalk and stopped the lathered up animal. Chandler halted his own mount beside his partner.

'Why'd you stop here, Jeb?' he asked.

The crimson light of a lamp covered in a red silk scarf tinted Foster as he dismounted and handed his long leathers to Chandler.

'Stay here a while,' Foster drawled.

'Where you going, Jeb?' Chandler asked as he rested his wrists on his saddle horn. 'You don't think Danvers is in one of the closest whore houses he happened to find, do you?'

Foster stepped on to the raised boardwalk.

'Nope. I do reckon that he must be familiar to all the folks in Diablo though.' Foster sighed as he struck a match and ignited the cigar he had just placed in the corner of his mouth. He blew smoke at the black sky and then tossed the match at the sand. 'Somebody might have seen the bastard and knows which way he was headed.'

Chandler watched as Foster stepped into the open doorway and entered the brothel. As with all men of his dubious occupation, Chandler was always aware of everything that was going on around him. Where most men calmly ignored the goings on which did not concern them, he had been trained to never relax. He knew that every man or woman who passed him were potential killers.

He tipped his hat brim at the dubious females as they walked along the boardwalk with the same grace he showed to the finest ladies back East. Yet he knew that no matter how pretty they might be, they were not to be taken for granted.

After what seemed like an eternity, he heard Foster's boots as they hurriedly descended the wooden staircase just beyond the door. He watched as his partner came out of the red brick structure and accepted his reins from Chandler.

'Danvers passed here about an hour back,

131

Lane.' Foster informed his partner as he gripped his saddle horn and mounted the exhausted horse. 'A few of the females said that a half-dozen customers started brawling upstairs. A big fight spilled out into the street just as Danvers was riding back into town. They collided with his grey.'

Chandler frowned as they turned their horses away from the scarlet illuminated building.

'Are you telling me that this Danvers critter killed all them men over there?' he queried, pointing back at the bodies which were strewn across the sand. 'What would he wanna do that for, Jeb?'

'The girls said it was a good fight so most of them piled down the stairs and watched,' Foster began. 'Danvers kinda got tangled up in the fight. They were crashing into his tall grey and that riled him up.'

'And he shot them?' Chandler gasped.

Foster gave a slow nod of his head. 'And he shot them. Shot them all dead. It seems that Danvers don't ration his anger on just town sheriffs, Lane. He'll shoot and kill anyone who gets in his way.'

'Where did he head after he killed them boys?'

Foster pointed.

'Right into the middle of Diablo.' He sighed.

Chandler exhaled. 'I'm tending to get mighty worried about Holt Danvers, partner. It seems that this is one critter we'll have to kill before he kills us.'

'You're right, Lane. This is one varmint I'm not going to even try and capture. Danvers has gotta be killed just like they reckoned back at headquarters,' Foster agreed.

Both horsemen tapped their spurs and started their horses walking again toward the very centre of the still busy town.

It could have been noon by the amount of light which cascaded on to the streets of Diablo as Holt Danvers stepped out from Joe Barnaby's office and stood counting the wad of money in his hands. A wry smile etched his features as he pulled out his wallet and inserted the crisp bills between its leather flaps. He returned the wallet to the inside pocket of his coat and patted it against his chest.

His eyes flashed as they surveyed every passing person in the crowded street. None of them had paid any heed to the shot he had just fired in Barnaby's office. Guns were being fired every few minutes in the lawless settlement and one more shot drew no more attention than the moths which fluttered around the street lamps.

Danvers adjusted his jacket. The wallet was swollen far more than it ought to have been but that was because he had just emptied Barnaby's safe of its entire contents.

Holt Danvers was a man who had decided that he was tired of playing games with the untrustworthy Barnaby. The fat man who had tried once too often to end his life.

The hired gunman had waited until Barnaby had dialled the combination into the safe's tumblers and opened the heavy metal door to withdraw the bonus money he had promised to pay Danvers when the notion came to the lethal gunsmith.

It was far more profitable to shoot Barnaby in the back of his fat head as he knelt counting his money, than it was to accept another job from him. So that was what Danvers had done. He had drawn one of his six-shooters and fired a perfectly placed bullet into the fat man as he rested on his knees before the iron safe.

Barnaby had made the mistake of thinking that as Danvers had been sitting in the adjacent room, he was safe. The distance was no problem for Danvers. His deadly accuracy with his .45 made shooting at a kneeling target twenty feet from him quite easy.

Then the tall hired killer had simply walked to the open safe and withdrawn every greenback from its belly. Most of the bills were hundreds.

The humourless Danvers inhaled the stale air and pulled the door shut behind the tails of his long dust coat. There was no remorse for killing Barnaby as he turned on his heels and started to walk back in the direction of the Buckhorn. As he gathered pace he wondered why he had waited so long to send the fat man back to his maker.

Joe Barnaby might have paid well enough but his habit of hiring younger outlaws to try and save himself from paying out the bonus money he owed had been his undoing. The fat old man had pushed his luck once too many times.

There were plenty of other rich men in Diablo who would hire someone of Danvers's infamous skills. Most would never dream of trying to kill rather than pay him his money.

A carriage trundled passed and then Danvers crossed the street. He stepped up on to the board-walk and pulled out his golden hunter. He pressed the winder and watched as its casing sprang open to reveal the time. He closed the lid and carefully wound the time-piece before sliding it back into his vest pocket. It was a habit which he had adopted several years before when he had observed the original owner checking the time just before he had killed him.

As his long legs returned him to his favourite drinking hole, he caught sight of his grey mare across the street. He had completely forgotten about the trail weary horse.

The animal was the most expensive thing he had ever purchased with his blood money. A vital expense all good killers could never be without.

He raised his gloved hand and rested it on the swing doors and stared in through the tobacco smoke at the still full saloon. The body was still where he had left it at the foot of the staircase but the patrons were simply enjoying themselves by moving around it. Danvers was about to push the doors inward when he saw the back of his glove glisten in the lantern light.

'Blood,' he whispered under his breath.

It was the blood of Joe Barnaby. Blood which had exploded from the front of the kneeling man's face and splattered all over the interior of the safe.

Danvers turned away from the saloon, stepped down on to the sand and strode quickly to where his horse was still tethered beside the water trough. He dipped his hand into the water and then rubbed the gore off the tight fitting leather.

His eyes narrowed as he straightened back up and stared at the weary mare. He patted the neck of the faithful horse and pulled its long leathers free of the hitching pole. Danvers was still thirsty but would wait until he had stabled his grey in the livery at the end of the long street.

'C'mon, horse,' the hired killer said before leading his horse away from the hotel and toward the livery stable. 'I'd better make sure you get tended and rested up in case we got us some hard riding to do.'

FOURTEEN

There was something about lawmen which Zococa
had always been able to recognize, no matter how
hard they tried to hide their tin stars from eagle-
eyed observers. He pulled back on his reins and
stopped his high-shouldered pinto stallion as he
led Tahoka into the brightest part of Diablo. Both
horsemen sat and watched as Foster and Chandler
drew up outside the famed Buckhorn.

'Look, Tahoka,' the famed bandit said as he
watched the two government agents. 'They are
unlike the other men we have met in Diablo. They
are uneasy.'

The large Indian gave a firm nod of his head.
His hooded eyes could also detect the difference
in their body language to that of the rest of
Diablo's menfolk.

The bandit leaned back against his silver cantle and straightened his sombrero. He watched the two government agents with a mixture of interest and amusement. Foster and Chandler dismounted and tethered their leathers around a weathered hitching pole before stepping up on to the board-walk.

They were obviously nervous as they looked around the area outside the still hectic saloon. While others were enjoying the dubious benefits that Diablo had to offer, Foster and Chandler were troubled.

Zococa watched as the agents entered the noisy saloon. He turned to his partner and raised his eyebrows.

'Those must be the gringos that the big black-smith in Silver Creek told us about, my little elephant,' Zococa said as he placed a long thin cigar between his teeth and scratched a match with his thumbnail.

Tahoka spoke with his fingers and hands.

'You doubt the great Zococa?' the bandit asked the mute Apache as he sucked in smoke and then blew out the match. 'Have I ever been wrong, *amigo*?'

Tahoka nodded.

'You cut me with your chattering, little one.'

Zococa grinned as he leaned over the ornate saddle horn and wondered why the pair of quiet lawmen were also hunting Danvers. 'We shall go and pay those gringos a visit, I think.'

Tahoka shook his head in disagreement and tried vainly to dissuade his partner from his daring venture. Zococa simply shook his head and waved a finger under the warrior's nose.

'Silence, my cautious one,' the bandit said. 'We have to find out why those men have come so far in search of the devil Danvers.'

Tahoka reluctantly sighed and nodded. They slapped their reins and encouraged their mounts to walk between the constant traffic that filled the street toward the saloon. The powerful pinto snorted as it slowly approached the two saddle horses at the saloon's hitching pole.

Zococa halted his stallion next to the agents' mounts and shook his head at the sight of the exhausted animals.

'These are very weary horses, *amigo*. Not like our precious mounts.' He sighed as he puffed on his flavoursome cigar. 'They have had a hard ride from Silver Creek with little rest.'

Tahoka leaned forward and caught sight of both Chandler and Foster in the smoke-filled saloon. He signalled to his partner that they were walking back out of the Buckhorn. He tapped his partner's sleeve. Zococa turned his head just as the government men pushed the swing doors apart and stepped back out onto the street.

Foster looked up at Zococa.

'You better not be too interested in our horse-flesh, friend,' he warned. 'We don't like varmints that pay too much heed to our nags. Savvy?'

Zococa gripped the cigar between his teeth and smiled at the two dust-caked men. He gave a nod at them.

'Do not fret, *amigo*.' He laughed. 'The great Zococa does not make glue. Your horses are quite safe.'

Chandler gripped his partner's arm and moved closer to Foster. Although there had never been a photographic likeness of the bandit, his description was well known.

'I recognize these two, Jeb,' he whispered. 'I've heard of a fancy Mexican bandit named Zococa and his big Apache pal. They're wanted dead or alive.'

Before Foster could reply, Tahoka drew his six-gun and aimed it at the pair. Both men started to raise their hands when Zococa shook his head.

'Do not raise your arms, *amigo*s,' he advised. 'That is something lawless men in Diablo never do. Are you the men who purchased horses back at

Silver Creek?'

'What if we are?' Foster growled.

'You are lawmen?' Zococa leaned down from his high-shouldered pinto so that his words were not overheard.

Neither Foster nor Chandler knew what to say. They feared that the truth might bring their lives to a premature end.

'Do not worry, *amigos*.' Zococa filled his lungs with smoke and looked into the eyes of the government men. 'We shall not hurt you. I think we have something in common.'

'If you ain't gonna hurt us then how come the Injun has got his gun aimed at us?' Chandler wondered.

'Tahoka is just making sure that you do not hurt us,' Zococa grinned. 'I ask you again, are you lawmen?'

Foster nodded. 'We're government agents. We've got orders to put an end to Holt Danvers, one way or another.'

Tahoka shook his head.

Zococa pulled the cigar from his lips and tapped the ash with his middle finger. 'Tahoka is not happy. He wants to kill Danvers himself.'

Foster stepped closer to the edge of the board-walk.

'What exactly do you want, Zococa?' he asked. 'Are you gonna tell your fellow outlaws about us? I'll bet you'd get a real kick out of seeing us lynched.'

The flamboyant bandit looked offended for a few brief moments before his smile returned to his face. 'You misjudge me, *amigo*. I know why Tahoka and myself are here to kill the evil Danvers but do not understand why you are—'

'We're just following orders, Zococa,' Chandler interrupted. 'Orders from Washington D.C.'

'I was wondering why two gringos who are obviously lawmen are in Diablo hunting the same hired killer as we are.' Zococa stared through his cigar smoke. 'Don't you know how dangerous it is for your breed in this town?'

Foster stepped closer to the pinto. 'We know exactly how dangerous a town like Diablo can be to men of our profession. What's your point?'

Zococa spoke with his fingers and the Apache warrior lowered his six-shooter before holstering it.

'You will never escape alive if you kill Danvers in Diablo, *amigo*,' he told the law officer. 'But if you work with Tahoka and myself, we shall ensure that you are able to return to this place you call Washington D.C.'

Chandler joined Foster at the edge of the weathered boards and brooded on the pact they had just been offered. It was a deal that neither of them had ever expected.

'It sounds like the solution we've been searching for, Jeb,' the agent said as he rubbed his whiskers thoughtfully.

Foster looked at his pal. 'These two hombres are wanted dead or alive on both sides of the border, Lane. How do we know we can trust them?'

'We don't but it's all we got.' Chandler looked at the haunting face of Tahoka before returning his attention to his partner. 'Besides, he's right. We ain't got a chance in hell of escaping this town alive without them.'

Reluctantly and against his better judgement, Foster nodded in agreement as he looked up at the still smiling bandit.

'You got a deal, Zococa,' he said with a sigh.

'This is very wise, *amigos*.' Zococa nodded and then swung his large mount around. He held the powerful stallion in check. 'Mount up. First we take our horses to the livery stable where they can be pampered, then we start our search for the evil Danvers.'

Both Chandler and Foster mounted their horses and backed them away from the hitching pole.

144

They looked at the colourful character with the cigar gripped between his teeth.

'How come you're so concerned about these nags?' Chandler wondered as he watched Tahoka turn his own sturdy mount. 'I'd have thought it was best if we just started looking for that hired killer.'

Zococa shook his head and glanced at the government agents. 'We need our horses refreshed after we have sent Danvers back to Hell, *amigos*. We might need them more than you think.'

'What do you mean by that?' Foster said as the four horsemen guided their animals through the still hectic street toward the fragrant livery stables. 'I thought you said that me and Lane would be safe after we dispose of Danvers.'

Zococa laughed out loud.

'*Sí, amigo*. I did say this but sometimes things do not go the way even the great Zococa plans,' he explained. 'Then it is wise to have rested horses you can flee upon.'

FIFTEEN

It wasn't too difficult to find the livery stable. Not only did its distinctive aroma point to its location but a tall beacon set just outside the tall weathered structure also drew more than its fair share of attention. Set upon a twelve foot tall pole just yards away from the entrance to the livery stable, a bowl of fiery coal oil sent massive flames up into the heavens, illuminating an otherwise dark part of Diablo.

Totally unaware that the man they were looking for was inside the wooden structure, the four riders slowly rode toward the stable as they each considered what they would do when they finally confronted the hired killer. Zococa was unusually quiet as they steered their mounts through the shadows toward the blazing torch. The Mexican bandit knew that his mute confederate Tahoka had already decided what the fate of Holt Danvers would be.

Even Zococa would be unable to prevent the Apache warrior from administrating his own brand of justice when they finally met up with Danvers. His handsome eyes darted to the two government agents as they rode beside Tahoka. Zococa realized that both of them were not in Diablo through choice and that meant they were unpredictable.

'There is the livery, *amigos*.' Zococa pointed his finger at the aromatic nightmare and shrugged. 'But I think your noses have already scented that.'

The ruthless Holt Danvers had stood with his knuckles resting upon his gun grips for nearly thirty minutes as the liveryman unsaddled his grey mare and carefully washed the sweating horse down. When satisfied that his precious mount was receiving the due care and attention he demanded, he nodded and turned away.

'You headed off to see Joe Barnaby now, Holt?' the curious liveryman asked as he dried his soapy hands along the sides of his pants. 'I bet that old coot owes you a few bucks.'

'Not any more he don't, Bobby.' Danvers stared

147

at Bob Berne and rasped as he checked his gold hunter for the umpteenth time.

'How come?'

'He's dead,' Danvers replied dryly, without looking at his inquisitor.

The liveryman gasped in shock. 'Joe's dead? Hell, how'd he die?'

Danvers glanced over his shoulder. 'I killed the bastard, that's how.'

There was a hushed silence for a few moments as the muscular man went about his business while Danvers stared with dead eyes out into the street. After drying the grey mare down and then tossing the towel aside, the liveryman cleared his throat and ventured.

'Where you off to now, Holt? The Buckhorn or to one of them fancy whore houses you favour?' he asked before leading the long-legged animal into a stall and hanging a feed bag over its head.

Danvers glanced back over his shoulder again and narrowed his eyes.

'You just look after that grey and you'll live a while longer, Bobby,' he warned.

The sweat-soaked man gave a fearful nod of his head. He did not have to be told a second time to keep his curiosity to himself. Even though Diablo was filled to the brim with wanted outlaws and equally dangerous bandits, none of them came close to the deadly Danvers for oozing sheer terror to those who set eyes upon him.

Suddenly the sound of horses' hoofs filled the vast interior of the high-sided stable. Both men looked at one another before Danvers swung on his boot heels and started to nod. Now it was his turn to be curious.

More than one rider was approaching the livery stable. He flicked the safety loops off both his holstered .45s and then gave a frightening smile.

'I wonder who that is, Bobby?' he muttered as the large man vanished into the shadows in search of cover. 'Reckon I'd best go greet them just in case they're hankering to be killed.'

The gunman walked through the wide open doors of the tall building and saw the four riders approaching. The towering bowl of flames above him cast eerily uncanny waves of light down the long narrow street.

For a brief moment Danvers had no idea who they were and then his cold calculated mind gave him the answer. He recognized the flamboyant Mexican astride the high-shouldered pinto stallion and the massive Indian who rode beside him. They were the two men who had been riding through the distant canyon after he had slain Frank Carver.

Something did not make any sense to the hired killer as he watched the four riders continue their approach. Danvers tilted his head as his fingers curled around his holstered gun grips. He did not believe what he was looking at, for it seemed impossible.

'What's going on here?' the merciless killer asked himself as his eyes burned through the smoke filled air. 'I killed that fancy Mexican already. I shot him clean through the heart. I seen him knocked off that pinto by the force of my rifle bullet. He can't be alive. Nobody can get plugged like that and still be alive.'

For the first time in his entire life, Holt Danvers was confused and it shook him to his marrow. He stepped close to the large barn door and pressed his shoulder against it. He poked his head around the rim of the door and looked again at the four horsemen.

'That is the same fancy Mexican,' he mumbled as he drew both his fully loaded six-shooters from their holsters and cocked them.

As the four horses slowly walked to where the flaming beacon stood just before the livery, Tahoka swiftly drew his Winchester and cranked its mechanism. A casing flew from the rifle's magazine.

'What is wrong, little one?' Zococa asked as he held his pinto in check and looked at his large companion.

Tahoka gave a forward nod of his head as his hooded eyes stared straight ahead. The large Apache threw his leg over the neck of his sturdy mount and slid to the ground. That was all Zococa needed to know. His mute friend had the honed instinct of a cougar.

'Dismount, *amigos*,' the bandit told the bewildered government agents. 'My little elephant has seen something.'

Jeb Foster listened to the warning and jumped from his saddle at the same time as Zococa. Both men crouched in the shadows of their horses as Chandler remained on his horse and peered ahead.

'I don't see anything, Jeb.'

That was the last thing Lane Chandler would ever say. The agent was about to reluctantly dismount when the quiet street shook with the deafening sound of gun shots as Danvers opened up on them.

Foster watched in horror as Chandler fell backward as his mount bolted. Droplets of blood marked his passage over his saddle cantle. As his dead body crashed into the sand a crimson shower of sickening gore followed him.

Their mounts raced after the saddle horse, leaving the three remaining men crouched on the ground beside what was left of Lane Chandler.

Zococa waved his drawn pistol. 'Spread out, *amigos.*'

Foster ran to the left side of the street in search of a shadow big enough to hide in until he gathered his wits and managed to see something to shoot back at. As his backbone hit a wall and he managed to pull his .45 free of its holster, he looked back at the remains of his partner. Then he noticed that both Zococa and the huge Tahoka had gone. He looked all around the narrow confines of the street but could not see either of them.

Suddenly more shots rang out. Foster glanced back at the stable and caught a glimpse of gun smoke hanging on the night air. He fired madly at the smoke and saw chunks of the livery door being hit by his bullets.

Danvers turned and moved back inside the livery. There were too many of them for his liking and he knew that he had to lure them inside the weathered structure if he was going to be able to ambush them. As he backed up his eyes looked up at the two lanterns which hung on chains from the rafters.

He was determined not to be betrayed by the circles of light which cast down and illuminated the centre of the livery. Danvers raised the gun in his left hand and fired two shots in quick succession.

The sound of shattering glass filled the livery as nervous horses bemoaned the disturbance to their peaceful rest. The interior of the huge structure was suddenly enveloped by darkness. Only the flickering golden glow of the torch light beyond the wide open doors gave Danvers any cause for concern.

He moved to the back of the stalls and positioned himself in a vacant one. Smoke drifted up from his guns as he screwed up his eyes and stared at the doors.

If anyone dared try to follow him into the livery he was ready to send them to the same place he had already dispatched Chandler to. A cruel grin filled his face as he studiously observed the torch lit entrance.

'C'mon, boys,' he hissed like a rattler. 'C'mon, get it.'

Then two shadows flashed across the entrance of the livery and traced across the interior of the walls. Danvers raised both his weapons and aimed them at the lantern-lit exterior and gritted his teeth.

'Who are you, *señor*?' Zococa's voice called out. 'Are you the bushwhacker they call Danvers?'

Danvers face twisted up in fury.

'My name's Holt Danvers,' he shouted.

'I am Zococa,' the bandit called out and moved stealthily toward the livery doors with his pistol gripped firmly in his hand. He watched as Foster reached the other side of the entrance and gave the agent a nod.

Suddenly both men raced into the darkness. They had barely entered when Danvers unleashed his guns at them. Zococa felt a bullet catch his sombrero and tear it from his head. As he staggered off balance and went to return fire, he saw Foster crumple beside him and fall on to his knees.

Not wishing to wait for the wounded Foster to get riddled with more of Danvers's bullets, Zococa threw himself across the sand and knocked Foster to the ground a fraction of a heartbeat before a volley of deafening lead cut through the air just over their heads.

The bandit fired his pistol to where he had seen the bright flashes of gunfire but all his shots found was the wooden wall supports. Then Zococa heard something above them as hefty footsteps crossed the loft above him.

It had to be Tahoka, he thought. His giant

Apache friend had climbed up to the loft and was making his way to where he could position himself above the deadly Danvers.

As the light from the fiery beacon danced across the back wall of the livery, Zococa caught a glimpse of Tahoka as he dropped on top of Danvers. It was a magnificent sight.

Then Zococa heard a scream.

It was the most chilling noise he had ever heard. As Zococa shielded Foster with his own body he heard more screams coming from out of the darkness. Only occasionally did the amber light capture the fighting men as they crashed through the wooden boards from one stall to another. Danvers attempted to defend himself against the powerful warrior but it was useless. Even his guns could not prevent Tahoka's unarmed onslaught as the Apache swatted the .45s out of the hired killer's hands as though they were annoying flies.

Desperately, Danvers threw a clenched fist and caught the expressionless Tahoka cleanly on the jaw but it only enraged the giant Indian even more. The warrior grappled with the stunned and dazed Danvers as though he were little more than a rag doll.

To even his amazement, Zococa watched as the massive Tahoka raised Danvers above his head as if he weighed little more than a feather. Then mustering every ounce of his incredible strength, Tahoka threw Danvers at the back wall of the livery stable. The Apache warrior moved into the shadows and then dropped down upon his stunned opponent.

There were no more screams. Just the sound of breaking bones as Tahoka made good his promise to snap the bushwhacker's neck.

Zococa helped Foster to his feet and pressed a hand against the savage bullet wound in his shoulder. The government agent panted breathlessly as Tahoka emerged from the shadows and paused beside his partner. He spoke briefly with his gigantic hands.

'What did he say, Zococa?' Foster asked.

'My little elephant said that the evil Danvers will never again make a little child an orphan, *amigo*,' Zococa answered.

FINALE

The sun was high and beat down upon the adobe mission as both Zococa and his silent friend rode across the arid sand toward San Maria. As they guided their mounts through the open gates of the mission, they were greeted by the elderly Father Joseph as he walked in his sun-bleached robes toward them. The monk watched as both horsemen dismounted and walked toward him.

Zococa held his large sombrero across his middle as the large Indian towered over him. The bandit hesitated to ask the monk about the small child, for he feared that he and Tahoka had discovered her broken body too late.

Father Joseph placed a hand upon the bandit's shoulder and smiled. It was the answer both he and Tahoka wanted.

'Mary is well, my son,' the monk gently said. 'She is a fighter. We mended her broken bones but even we cannot mend the sadness she feels. The brothers took a wagon to the canyon and brought back her father's body for burial.'

'Where is Señor Carver buried, Father?' Zococa asked.

Father Joseph pointed to the garden oasis beside the chapel. Both Zococa and Tahoka could see the small child in a wheelchair close to a rose bush and a wooden cross.

'She spends many hours there each day, my son.'

Zococa lowered his sombrero and revealed a newly purchased doll. He handed it to his lumbering friend and smiled at Tahoka.

'Take the doll to Mary, *amigo*,' he said.

Reluctantly the Apache brave took hold of the doll and walked nervously toward the small child. Zococa then reached into his coat pocket and withdrew a thick pile of bank notes and gave them to Father Joseph.

'Where did you get this, my son?' the monk asked as he frowned at the bandit. 'This is not stolen money, is it?'

Zococa smiled and pulled out his dented silver cigar case.

'No, Father.' He grinned as he produced a slim black cigar from its gleaming interior. 'We did not steal this money. We found it in the pocket of the evil man who killed Mary's father. We decided to give it to you to help the mission and the child.'

Both men turned and watched as the gentle giant knelt before the child and nervously handed her the doll. She beamed at Tahoka and clutched the doll to her chest. Her happiness washed over them.

'That is the first time since she awoke from her injuries that Mary has smiled, Zococa.' Father Joseph sighed. 'I thank you both for that.'

Zococa ignited a match with his thumbnail and sucked smoke into his lungs as he nodded. He then raised an eyebrow and glanced at the cloud-less heavens.

'We had a little help, *amigo*,' he admitted.